SPRING SHOW SEASON AT WILLOWCREEK

AN EQUESTRIAN WOMEN'S FICTION NOVEL OF HEALING, RIVALRY, AND LIFE AT A RURAL STABLE

(THE WILLOW CREEK SEASONS) BOOK TWO

LAURA ASHWOOD

CONTENTS

Prologue — v

Chapter 1 — 1
Chapter 2 — 21
Chapter 3 — 44
Chapter 4 — 53
Chapter 5 — 60
Chapter 6 — 65
Chapter 7 — 72
Chapter 8 — 93
Chapter 9 — 97
Chapter 10 — 101
Chapter 11 — 105
Chapter 12 — 109

Coming Soon — 115
Behind the Scenes at Willow Creek — 117
Clara's Show Day Calming Cookies — 121

PROLOGUE

Spring sunlight warmed the valley in a way that felt almost like forgiveness. It touched the tops of the maples first, then the dripping roofs of the old barns, then the layered fields where winter had finally loosened its stubborn grip. Snowmelt slipped in silver runnels toward the creek, carrying bits of last year's leaves along the way. Calves bawled on distant hillsides, their cries echoing across the quiet morning. Everywhere, green pushed through the thaw, tender and determined.

Willow Creek Stables breathed again.

Clara Bennett stood outside the barn with her hands in her coat pockets, boots planted in thawing earth that released the faint scent of mud and frost and new life. She closed her eyes and let the sun warm her cheeks. It felt like the first true warmth of the season. The kind of warmth that said the world was ready to move forward again, and maybe she was too.

Behind her, the barn door creaked. Aspen's soft whicker drifted out like a greeting.

"I know," Clara said as she turned toward the sound. "It feels different today."

The gray mare poked her head over the stall gate, breath swirling in little clouds. Her coat had begun to shed in uneven tufts, mottling the clean silver with patches of darker winter hair. Clara brushed a few strands from her sleeve. The air hummed with quiet life: the rustle of hay, the drip of melting ice, the hum of insects brave enough to emerge early.

Winter at Willow Creek had changed her. She had arrived worn down, afraid to ride again, aching from memories she could not quiet. She had not chased applause in those months. She had chased something far quieter. The rightness of a stall door sliding open. The comfort of Aspen's breath against her cheek. The sound of her father's voice drifting across the kitchen. Luke's steady presence, never demanding, always there.

And now here she stood, preparing for something she had once sworn she might never face again.

Their first show since the accident.

She drew her coat closer and let her gaze travel over the familiar landscape. The practice arena lay just beyond the paddock, its sand newly dragged, the rails waiting to be set. Beyond it, the rolling hills glowed under the sun, dotted with stone walls and last year's grass. Nothing had changed, and yet everything had.

Clara took a slow breath. She did not want applause this time. She wanted proof that courage could be quiet and lasting. The kind that took root inside you slowly, the way spring crept into the valley.

Footsteps approached from the gravel. Luke Hayes crossed the yard with gloves tucked into his back pocket and a coil of lead rope slung over one shoulder. His gaze found hers immediately, steady and warm in the morning light.

"Fence line is dry," he said. "Good footing for later."

Clara nodded. "I thought the same. It feels like a good day."

"It is," he said, and his voice held something gentle that settled inside her like a warm stone. "Everything looks ready."

He stood beside her, both of them facing the fields. For a moment they said nothing. The quiet between them was easy. Familiar. A soft place she had not known she needed until he offered it.

"You slept?" he asked.

"Better than usual," Clara said. "The worry kept circling for a while, but it never took hold."

"That is a good sign."

She smiled. "Maybe."

Snow still clung to the shadowed edges of the paddock, but the center was soft and open. A few birds swooped low across the yard as if celebrating the return of warmth. Far off, the creek rushed with spring melt, running fast and bright enough to catch the sunlight.

Luke leaned on the fence rail. "You do not have to prove anything to anyone but yourself."

"I know," Clara said quietly. "But I need to know I can do this without falling apart."

"You already have," Luke said. "Everything after this is practice."

A warmth pressed behind her ribs. She did not know how to answer. Instead she let her hand brush a piece of frost from the top rail and watched it melt instantly on her palm.

They walked to the barn together. Maggie was already inside, a messy bun perched on her head and bright spring lipstick smudged slightly from rushing. She held a clipboard under one arm and a mug of coffee in her other hand.

"Today is a big day," Maggie said. "Regional warm-up packet should arrive any minute. I made muffins. Apple cinnamon. Motivation muffins."

Clara laughed. "You are more excited than I am."

"I have to balance your calmness somehow," Maggie said. "Otherwise this whole family would drift into quiet introspection and never come out."

Tom emerged from the tack room with a permanent-marker label stuck to his shirt. He peeled it off and slapped it onto a metal bin. "I organized all the show supplies," he announced. "I found three bottles of hoof oil we did not know we had."

Maggie blinked. "Dad, that is the most optimistic thing you have said all week."

Tom pretended not to smile. "A barn cannot function without inventory."

Clara listened to them, heart swelling with something that felt dangerously close to joy. Last year she would have missed moments like this. She would have been somewhere far away, consumed with training schedules and sponsor expectations and the endless ache of wanting to be perfect. Now she stood in a barn that smelled like home, surrounded by people who wanted nothing more than for her to be whole.

And maybe she was on her way.

The practice arena felt alive when they walked out together. Rakes had carved neat waves through the soft sand. The bright fences stood in careful rows, waiting. The sun warmed Clara's shoulders as she mounted Aspen. The mare lifted beneath her with an energy that made Clara's chest loosen.

They circled the arena in a slow walk. Aspen's ears twitched toward the fences. The rhythm of hoofbeats steadied Clara's breathing. The winter had been full of slow rides and careful steps. This was different. This was a return.

"Ready?" Luke asked from the gate.

Clara nodded. "I think so."

She asked Aspen to trot. The mare moved forward with smooth eagerness, her stride opening with each lap. Clara posted softly, letting herself settle into the movement. Her shoulder felt steady. Her mind felt steady. The winter training had rebuilt trust one quiet day at a time.

"Set the poles," Maggie said, already jogging to adjust a rail. "Let her see something bright."

Clara guided Aspen toward the small vertical. Red rails. Clean lines. Nothing threatening. She breathed out long and low.

"Easy," she said.

The canter rolled out of Aspen like water. The first fence

approached. It came to them without rush or hesitation, just a single note sung perfectly on pitch. The second fence flowed the same way. At the third, a bird burst from the hedgerow. Clara's pulse jolted. A memory flashed: the roar of a summer crowd, Aspen stumbling, the ground rushing up.

Her grip tightened. But then she softened her elbow deliberately and breathed deep through her chest. Aspen listened. The landing came soft. Balanced. Almost boring in its steadiness.

A miracle disguised as ordinary work.

Luke's voice carried from the gate. "That looked right. Again when you are ready."

Clara slowed Aspen to a walk. The spring light washed the arena in soft gold. The barn roof gleamed in the distance, bright above the first blush of green. Everything felt clear. Open. Possible.

That was when the courier truck turned at the lane.

The tires spit dust from the gravel. Maggie saw it first and sprinted toward the porch, dropping her clipboard on the ground. Clara watched her sister wave at the driver, accept a packet the size of a magazine, and run toward the arena with eyes wide.

Maggie reached them breathless. "It came. Regional schedule. And a personal note from the director. They saw the video of your winter rides. They are excited to see you back."

Clara's heart stumbled.

She took the envelope. It felt heavier than paper had any right to feel. Inside was the full season schedule. Warm-up dates. Class lists. Maps. A handwritten line at the bottom of the welcome page:

We are glad you are riding again. Welcome back to the arena.

A warmth spread through Clara so slowly she almost did not notice it at first. Luke stepped close, laying one hand on Aspen's bridle. His thumb moved in a small circle on the leather, almost unconsciously.

"Well," he said softly. "Looks like show season is calling."

Clara looked at the letter. Then at the bright fences. Then at Aspen, who had carried her through winter storms and fear and the long road home. The wind lifted a strand of Clara's hair and brushed it across her cheek. Somewhere, far off, the loudspeaker at the county fairgrounds tested a tone. It rose into the air, steady and clear, then faded like a promise.

Something clicked inside her. Quiet but final. A small truth finding the right track.

"It is time," she said.

Aspen arched her neck as if she understood. The sunlight caught along her mane like a silver ribbon. Clara felt the moment settle deep in her chest, a beginning wrapped inside a decision.

She had returned to the arena. Not for applause. Not for anyone else's expectations.

For herself.

Because courage, she now knew, could be quiet and strong and hers alone.

And every season brought a new test. A new challenge. A new chance to ride toward home.

1

The first warm breeze of spring slipped over the valley and carried the smell of thawed earth to the front porch.

Clara Bennett paused with one boot on the step and closed her eyes. The air felt soft against her cheeks, nothing like the sharp winter wind that had chased her shoulders up around her ears for months. Somewhere down the hill, the creek murmured over stones, louder than it had in weeks. A crow called once from the bare branches of the old maple tree, then launched itself across the pale sky.

"Clara, honey, you will miss your ride time if you stand there breathing," her mother called from inside the house. Her voice was light, teasing, but there was the familiar edge beneath it. Worry, carefully disguised as humor.

"I am going," Clara answered, even though her heart was beating a little too fast for someone who was just going to the barn. She opened her eyes and forced her foot to move. The wooden steps creaked, and a small patch of dampness soaked through the sole of her boot. The snow in the front yard had finally given way to patches of flattened, yellowed grass and dark soil.

It was just another day at Willow Creek Stables. That was what she told herself. Not the first full training ride since the accident. Not a test.

Just another day.

The truck's engine coughed when she turned the key, then caught. She let it warm up while she stretched her fingers around the steering wheel, flexing them as if they were stiff from cold rather than nerves. When she glanced back at the house, her mother was framed in the kitchen window, one hand wrapped around a mug, the other lifting in a small wave.

Clara waved back. It was easy from this distance. Up close, she still saw flashes of her mother's face from the night of the accident, lit by barn floodlights, pale and frightened.

She backed down the driveway, the gravel crunching. The valley opened in front of her, fields rolling out in soft curves. The distant hills were still patched with snow, but the lower pasture fences cut sharp lines across damp, dark ground. A small herd of calves clustered near their mothers in one of the fields, little ears twitching at the morning.

The sun sat low over the ridge but it had warmth in it now. Meltwater glimmered in the ditches that ran alongside the road. As the truck bumped along, Clara let herself look toward the far side of the valley.

There, sitting on its rise above the creek, stood Willow Creek Stables.

The red barn roofs glowed against the washed-out sky. White fences traced neat rectangles around the turnout paddocks. The indoor arena roof still wore a thin, sluggish layer of snow that was sliding away in dirty streaks. The outdoor arenas, though, were bare and dark, the footing soaked with recent melt, waiting.

Waiting for them.

Clara's stomach tightened. She pulled into the gravel lot, where puddles flashed like mirrors. A couple of cars and a horse trailer were already parked. The familiar sounds reached her even before she opened the door. A horse somewhere inside the barn banged a hoof against a stall wall. Another snorted, deep and impatient. Someone laughed. A radio crackled faintly with country music.

Normal barn noises. Ordinary.

Her hands still trembled a little as she cut the engine.

Clara climbed out and stood for a moment, letting the warmth of the sun press against her back through her jacket. The smell of hay, manure, and leather drifted from the open barn doors, touched with something fresher now: wet earth, spring air, the faint sweet scent of the first grass daring to poke through.

A sudden burst of squealing from the far pasture made her head snap up. Two yearlings were racing the fence line, tails flagged, legs flying in uneven, joyful strides. Beyond them, in a smaller field close to the barn, two mares grazed near their foals. The foals were still fuzzy and clumsy, their legs too long for their bodies. One of them took a few stiff, exaggerated steps, then gave a tiny buck as if surprised by its own power.

The sight loosened something in Clara's chest. She smiled without meaning to.

"Hey, stranger." The voice came from her left.

She turned to see Harper coming toward her across the lot, helmet already in hand, dark hair in a messy braid that had escaped from its tie. A smear of something green marked the sleeve of her jacket. Probably aloe gel from bandaging a horse. Or a smear of green hoof dressing. With Harper, it was hard to tell.

"You are early," Clara said, stuffing her hands into her pockets to hide their shake. "Or did I get the time wrong?"

"You are right on time." Harper bumped her shoulder lightly against Clara's. "I am just obsessed with this weather. I got here before sunrise just to smell the arena."

"That is not weird at all," Clara said, the corners of her mouth tugging higher even as her pulse thudded unevenly. "Not even a little."

"Wait until I tell you the part where I hugged a jump standard." Harper grinned, then let her eyes roam over Clara's face. "You okay?"

The question was casual, but they both knew it was not casual.

Clara lifted one shoulder. "Nervous, I guess."

"Of course you are." Harper's voice softened. "First full ride. First lesson back with Luke that is not him making you walk in circles and talk about your feelings."

"He did not make me talk," Clara muttered.

"He did not have to. You glared and then told him everything anyway."

"That is not how I remember it."

"Selective memory," Harper said, but she did not push. "Come on. Aspen heard your truck. He has been pacing since dawn."

They walked toward the barn together. The big sliding doors stood open, and the familiar rectangle of shadow welcomed them in. As Clara crossed the threshold, the smell of the barn wrapped around her like a blanket. Hay. Dust. Sawdust. The sharpness of fresh shavings. The metallic hint of horseshoes on concrete.

For a moment, another memory flashed sensory-strong: the same smell mixed with something bitter, the screech of hooves on icy ground, the gut-deep thud when a body hit the earth. Her breath hitched.

Then the present rushed in again. A chestnut gelding stuck his head over the nearest stall door, ears pricked.

"Morning, Rocket," Harper said, scratching the horse's forehead as they passed.

The aisle was busy. Zoey carried a saddle down from the tack room, the leather creaking softly. Mr. Martinez, the farrier, knelt at a gray pony's hoof, rasp scraping rhythmically. A boarder swept shavings out of the aisle, humming along with the faint music from the radio.

Just another morning at Willow Creek.

"Clara." The voice came from farther down the aisle. Warm, steady.

She did not need to look to know it was Luke Hayes. She looked anyway.

He stood in front of Aspen's stall, one hand resting on the latch, the other wrapped around a coffee mug. His dark hair stuck out in places as if he had run his fingers through it too many times. His jacket hung open over a faded Willow Creek Stables hoodie. A smear of dust crossed one cheek.

"Hi," Clara said. The word felt too small for the moment.

Luke's eyes flicked over her quickly, taking in her posture, the set of her shoulders, her grip on her helmet. His gaze lingered, just for a second, on her jaw, where she knew the muscles were tight.

"Good timing," he said. "Aspen has been trying to dismantle his hay net waiting for you."

"I told you." Harper smirked. "Obsessed."

Clara stepped up to the stall door. Aspen was there, right on the other side, dark bay coat glossy even in the low light. His star shone white against his forehead. He lifted his head as she approached, ears pushing forward, eyes soft. The small scar at his shoulder, a faint line under the hair, was almost invisible now. Almost.

"Hey, boy," Clara whispered. She reached out and he pushed his muzzle into her palm, warm breath ghosting over her skin. His whiskers tickled, and he stretched his neck to nudge her shoulder, as if to say Where have you been.

"I know," she murmured. "I missed you too."

For a moment, everything else fell away. There was only the feel of his breath, the familiar grain of his forelock between her fingers, the steady sound of his chewing as he picked up another mouthful of hay. The tightness in her chest eased a little more.

"She thinks I am too fragile to trot," Clara said, without looking away from Aspen. The words came out lighter than she felt them.

"I think you are strong enough to be honest," Harper replied. "That is scarier."

"Harper is right," Luke said. "About both things."

"Do not agree with her," Clara said automatically. "It encourages her."

He smiled, just a small shift at the corner of his mouth. "You ready?" he asked.

Clara lifted her chin. "Yes."

The word surprised her. It came out with more certainty than she had expected. It felt good in her mouth.

Luke searched her face for another beat, then nodded once. "All right. Let us get him tacked up. We will keep it simple. Remember what we talked about."

"I know," she said again. "One stride at a time."

"And if something feels wrong?"

"I stop. I breathe. I talk to you."

"And?"

"And I do not pretend I am fine when I am not," she finished, making a face.

"Good," Luke said. "Because I am getting better at spotting that."

"You always were," Harper said. "He is like a human lie detector. It is extremely annoying."

Luke shook his head, but the warmth in his eyes did not dim. "Harper, you are on stall duty after your ride. We are pulling the last of the winter mats in the wash stalls."

"Yes, Captain," Harper said, snapping off a sloppy salute. Then she squeezed Clara's arm. "You got this. I will be spying from the rail."

"Great," Clara said. "No pressure."

Harper trotted off toward the tack room, leaving Clara and Luke with Aspen.

They moved through the familiar motions of tacking up. Clara slid the halter over Aspen's ears and clipped on the lead rope, then opened the stall and led him into the cross ties. He followed willingly, hooves ringing softly on the concrete.

She brushed him with long, even strokes, the curry comb lifting winter dust from his coat. Hair floated in the air like dull brown confetti. The rhythm soothed her. Grooming had been the one thing she could still do in the weeks after the fall, when the doctors had restricted her from riding. Standing beside Aspen, hands busy, mind quiet, she had learned the curves of his body all over again, as if reassuring herself he was still here, still whole.

"Looks good," Luke said, running a hand lightly over Aspen's back to check for tenderness. "How is your side?"

"Fine," Clara said automatically, then winced at herself. "Tight. Especially when I twist. But better than last month."

He nodded. "Remember to stretch before you get on. No heroics."

"I know," she said.

He raised an eyebrow, and she rolled her eyes. "I promise."

They saddled Aspen together, settling the pad carefully, slipping the saddle into place, tightening the girth slowly so he could adjust. Aspen flicked an ear but stood quietly, his dark eye flicking between them.

Every small sound in the barn seemed louder than usual. The clang of a dropped hoof pick. The thud of a bale of shavings in the next aisle. A boarder's laughter bouncing off the rafters. At one point, a wheelbarrow slammed into the wall when someone misjudged a turn. The noise cracked like a shot in the air.

Clara's whole body jerked. Her hand flew to Aspen's mane. Her heart spiked, breath stuttering.

"Sorry," a voice called from around the corner. "My bad."

"It is okay," Luke replied easily. His attention never left Clara. "You all right?"

She swallowed. The barn had shifted, just for a second. The dust motes in the air seemed brighter, the lights harsher. Her mind had flashed her back to the icy day, the horse slipping, the sick lurch of falling weight.

"I am fine," she said. The words came out too fast.

Luke did not call her on it. He just stepped closer, enough that she could feel the calm gravity of him beside her. "Name three things you see right now," he said quietly.

She wanted to protest that she did not need his exercises, but her pulse was still racing. "Aspen's star," she said, looking at the white patch on the gelding's forehead. "The mud on your boots. The reflection in that water bucket."

"Two things you can feel," he prompted.

"The brush in my hand." She tightened her fingers around it. "The leather of the saddle against my leg."

"One thing you can smell."

"Hay," she whispered. "Just hay."

"Good," Luke said. "You are here. Not there. That is all."

Her shoulders dropped an inch. Aspen blew out a breath and lowered his head, as if he had been holding tension too.

"Sorry," she said softly.

"For what?" Luke's voice stayed mild.

"For... I do not know. Jumping every time someone breathes too loudly," she muttered.

He shook his head. "You are recovering from something big. Your brain is doing its job trying to keep you safe. We just have to teach it that not every loud noise is a threat. That takes time."

"Time you do not have if you want me ready for the Spring Show," she said.

He gave her a look. "I did not say that. And we will talk about the show later. Today is about today."

"Everyone else is already talking about it," Clara said. "Zoey and Harper were arguing over which classes they were entering in the indoor. And I heard someone say we are getting new banners and jumps and everything. It is like the biggest thing to happen to Willow Creek this year."

Luke's mouth quirked. "It is a big deal. We have not hosted a show this size in a while. It will be good for the barn. New riders, new energy."

"New people to embarrass myself in front of," Clara said under her breath.

"You are not going to embarrass yourself," he said. "And for the record, we think the show will be even bigger than usual."

She glanced at him. "Why?"

He hesitated, as if deciding how much to say. "There has been talk about a possible sponsor coming out to watch. Nothing official yet. Just rumors. If it happens, it could be good for Willow Creek."

"A sponsor?" Clara repeated. The word sat oddly on her tongue. "Like... free saddle pads with logos and stuff?"

"And more," Luke said. "Prize money. Media coverage. Opportunities for riders. But like I said, it is only talk right now."

Her mind flicked back to the accident, to the way whispers had followed her through the winter. She did not like the idea of extra eyes on her. But she also pictured the barn, freshly painted, full of banners and bright jumps and proud horses, and something fluttered in her chest that was not entirely fear.

"Who is it?" she asked.

Luke shook his head. "I do not know. I think Hannah has more details, but she has not said much yet. She wants to get final confirmation before she gets everyone worked up."

"Too late," Clara said. "If Zoey finds out, she will plan her entire wardrobe around impressing this mystery sponsor."

"More reason not to tell her yet," Luke murmured. "Anyway, we can worry about that when it is real. For now, your seat is what we are working on, not your autograph."

She made a face at him but the tightness in her chest had eased again. "Fine. My seat. The least glamorous part of riding."

"The most important," he corrected. "All right. Finish that girth. Then you do your stretches in the indoor before you get on."

"Yes, sir," she said, mock-saluting.

He snorted softly and moved aside to let her work.

By the time she led Aspen toward the indoor arena, the barn aisle felt less like a tunnel and more like what it had always been: a path to something she loved.

The indoor doors stood half open, letting the watery sunlight spill onto the packed footing. The air inside still held some of winter's chill, but it did not chew into her bones the way it had in January. Dust floated in slanting beams of light. Someone had already dragged the arena, and the surface lay in smooth, even lines with only a few hoofprints breaking the pattern.

On the far wall, the course from last night's lesson still stood: a couple of crossrails, a small oxer, a line of poles on the ground, and a low vertical. Nothing higher than two feet. Nothing she and Aspen had not done a hundred times.

Clara stopped just inside the door and let Aspen stand while she did her stretches. She rolled her shoulders, then turned slowly side to side, feeling the tug around her ribs where bruised bone had healed. She reached for her toes and held the stretch until the back of her legs stopped complaining.

She did not look at the jumps yet. She focused on her body, the way it felt today, not the way it had felt on the day she fell. New day, she told herself. New footing. No ice. No wind.

When she straightened, Luke was there beside her, leaning on the arena railing. Harper perched next to him, chin on her hands, feet swinging.

"No pressure," Harper called. "We are only here to judge you."

"Very helpful," Clara said.

Aspen tossed his head, as if responding. She patted his neck. "Ignore her. She does not even know what diagonal she is on half the time."

"I will have you know I am now right on diagonals at least eighty percent of the time," Harper said. "Personal growth."

Luke chuckled. "Okay, Clara. You know the plan. Get on at the mounting block. We will start with a few laps at the walk. Then see how you feel."

She led Aspen to the mounting block, her heartbeat roaring in her ears. The block looked taller than usual. The stirrup seemed farther away. She placed one foot on the first step, then the second. Her hand shook when she caught the reins.

Aspen stood rock steady. Luke stepped closer, just within reach but not touching her.

"You have done this thousands of times," he said quietly.

"I have fallen once," she replied, just as quietly.

"And you got back up," he said. "Not in the saddle yet, but you did. You came back to the barn. You groomed. You hand walked. You sat on him at the halt when you were ready. All of that counts."

She swallowed. Her throat felt too tight for words, so she just nodded.

"Ready?" he asked.

She took a breath and nodded again.

She put her left foot in the stirrup. For a heartbeat, her body remembered the feeling of the world dropping out from under her. Her muscles tried to lock. She forced herself to move anyway, pushing up, swinging her right leg over Aspen's back, settling gently into the saddle.

The leather creaked. The familiar shape of the seat cradled her. Aspen flicked an ear back at her but did not move a hoof until she asked.

"I am up," she said.

She had not realized she was holding her breath until it came out in a rush.

Luke's shoulders eased minutely. "Good. Take a moment. Feel how he moves under you, just at the halt."

She did. She shifted her weight slightly left, then right. Aspen balanced beneath her without complaint. The contact of her calves against his sides felt foreign and yet so known that her chest ached.

Her fingers tightened on the reins, then relaxed. "He feels... okay."

"He feels like Aspen," Luke said. "When you are ready, walk on."

She clucked softly and squeezed with her calves. Aspen stepped forward, hooves whispering on the softened footing. His walk was long and swinging, his head and neck stretching as he sought contact. The movement rolled gently through her hips.

With every stride, her body remembered. Her mind still tried to offer images she did not want, but they were quieter, drowned out by the steady rhythm underneath her.

"Good," Luke called. "Just let him walk. Breathe with him. In for two steps, out for two."

She did as he said, inhaling as Aspen's left fore and right hind moved, exhaling as the other pair followed. The pattern settled into her, matching the beating of her heart until the two rhythms felt less at odds.

They walked large around the arena a few times. Harper clapped very quietly from the rail, as if applauding a delicate song.

"She is doing great," Harper muttered to Luke, loud enough that Clara could hear.

"She is," Luke said. "But we do not say that yet. We keep her focused."

"I can still hear you," Clara said.

"Good," Luke replied. "Then you know we are here. All right. Pick up a light contact. Let us do some big circles. Keep your eyes up."

They worked through the basics. Circles at the walk. Changes of direction. Serpentines along the long side. Luke's voice guided her, offering small corrections. "Open your inside rein. Support with your outside leg. Do not lean."

At first, every tiny wobble in Aspen's stride sent a spike of worry through Clara. Was he about to trip? Was the footing too slick? Was she sitting crooked and unbalancing him?

But he moved forward calmly, his ears flicking back and forth, listening. When a gust of wind rattled the arena roof, he only twitched an ear. When a door banged somewhere in the barn, he snorted once and kept walking.

He trusted her, even if a part of her did not trust herself.

After a while, Luke said, "How does your body feel?"

"Sore," she admitted. "But a good sore. Like the first day back at school after summer break."

"That is a metaphor I have not heard before," Harper said.

"You would not know," Clara shot back lightly. "You spent all summer last year at the barn instead of doing the reading list."

"And I still passed English," Harper said. "Talent."

"Back to riding, please," Luke said, but his tone was amused. "Clara, when you come across the diagonal, ask for a halt. Let us see if he is listening off your seat."

They practiced transitions: walk to halt, halt to walk, walk to a very slow almost-halt and then forward again. Each one reminded Clara that she was not just a passenger. She had tools, skills, ways to communicate with the horse beneath her that had nothing to do with panic or falling.

When Luke finally said, "I think you are ready to trot," her stomach dropped.

She knew this moment was coming. They had talked about it in the office, in carefully planned steps. But talking was one thing. Asking Aspen to lift into that bouncier gait, the one that mimicked the motion before a canter, before jumping, before everything that had gone wrong... that was another.

Her hands tightened on the reins.

"We do not have to," Luke said quietly. "Not today. We can stay at the walk and still call this a win."

If he had pushed, she might have dug in her heels just to prove she could. His willingness to let her stop made the fear stand out in stark relief.

She thought of all the nights she had lain in bed replaying the accident, imagining different outcomes, different choices. She thought of Aspen standing in his stall all winter, full of energy, patient and confused. She thought of the foals in the field, awkwardly learning to use their legs.

She did not want to be stuck in the moment of falling forever.

"I want to try," she said.

Luke nodded once. "Okay. Just a few strides. Down the long side. If at any point you feel overwhelmed, you come back to walk. That is not failure. That is smart riding."

"Right," she whispered.

She brought Aspen onto a twenty-meter circle at one end of the arena. The sand crunched softly under his feet. Her breathing quickened. She adjusted her seat, sitting a little deeper, closing her calves gently.

"Trot," she asked softly.

For a heartbeat, nothing happened. Then Aspen lifted into trot. The world changed texture, moving through her bones with a familiar, rolling bounce. Her balance wobbled once, twice, but she found it again, heels weighted, hands steady.

Her heart hammered, but not with the wild, spiraling panic she had expected. It was more like standing at the edge of a cold lake and finally plunging in. The shock of it, the bite of the water, and then the realization that she could still breathe.

"Good," Luke called, his voice steady and close. "There you go. Let him trot. Do not hang on his mouth. Breathe."

Harper whooped once, then clapped a hand over her mouth when Luke gave her a look.

Clara laughed, a slightly wild sound. It bubbled up from somewhere deep and shook free of her chest.

"Okay," Luke said after a few circles. "Back to walk."

She squeezed with her thighs, exhaled, and closed her fingers. Aspen obediently dropped back into a walk, ears flicking as if to ask That all.

She let the reins slip through her fingers a little, giving him his neck. Her legs were buzzing, both from the exertion and the fear.

"How do you feel?" Luke asked.

She searched for the answer. "Like my insides ran a marathon," she said. "But... good. I did not die."

"That is always a plus," Harper said.

"You did better than 'did not die,'" Luke said. "You rode. You made choices. You corrected him when he leaned. You posted on the right diagonal."

Clara blinked. "I did?"

He smiled. "Yes, you did."

She let that sink in like warm water through cold fingers. She had been so focused on not falling that she had not realized her body had slipped back into old habits of balance and timing.

"Can we trot again?" she asked suddenly.

He did not make a big deal of it. He just nodded. "Sure. Same deal. A few laps. Then we are done. Let us leave today on a good note."

The second trot was easier. Her muscles remembered faster. Her mind still offered flickers of fear when Aspen stumbled slightly on a deeper patch of footing, but the panic did not take over. She corrected her position, lifted his pace with a soft squeeze, and they moved on.

By the time they cooled out at the walk, sweat darkened Aspen's neck and a light sheen had formed on Clara's upper lip. She slumped slightly in the saddle, not from poor posture but from a bone-deep kind of exhaustion she had not expected. Emotional energy, drained.

Luke walked beside Aspen, hand resting lightly on the horse's shoulder. "That is enough for today," he said. "You did exactly what I hoped for."

"What did you hope for?" she asked.

"That you would give yourself a chance," he said simply.

Harper met them at the arena gate. "That was so good," she said. "How do you feel? On a scale of one to throwing up."

"Maybe a six," Clara said. "But trending toward five."

"One is no nausea, right?" Harper asked.

"Obviously."

"Then you are doing great."

They laughed, and the sound bounced off the arena walls in a way that felt like reclaiming territory.

Back in the barn aisle, Clara slid off Aspen carefully, using the mounting block again instead of swinging down to the concrete. Her knees wobbled when her feet hit the ground, and Aspen turned his head to nuzzle her shoulder.

"Traitor," she said fondly, scratching his forehead. "You liked trotting too much."

He snorted softly and sniffed at her hair.

"Walk him out and then give him a good groom," Luke said. "Light cool blanket if you think he needs it. Then you, young rider, go home and rest. No sneaking back for extra rides."

"What if I want to ride the foals?" she asked.

"Then I will send you back to the doctor," he said dryly. "You are not allowed near anything under three years old with your current decision-making."

She grinned. "Noted."

He started to walk away, then paused. "Clara."

She looked up.

"I am proud of you," he said.

He said it matter-of-factly, like he was noting the weather. That, more than anything, made her throat tighten again.

"Thanks," she said quietly.

When he disappeared toward the office, Harper drifted closer, looping an arm through Clara's as they walked Aspen up and down the aisle together.

"You know he is right," Harper said. "You were awesome."

"I was terrified," Clara said.

"You can be both," Harper replied. "Terrified and awesome. That is kind of your brand."

"Great," Clara said. "Exactly the brand I always wanted."

"Better than Zoey's brand, which is Dramatic with capital D," Harper said. "Speaking of, have you heard her latest theory about the Spring Show?"

Clara arched an eyebrow. "Do I want to?"

"She thinks we are going to have riders coming in from all over the state," Harper said. "Including a 'mysterious rider from someone's past.' Her words, not mine."

Clara frowned. "From whose past?"

"Who knows. She has been collecting gossip from the feed store and the tack shop like it is her job." Harper shrugged. "But Hannah did say we will have more out-of-town entries this year. Something about the show being part of a new regional circuit."

"Great," Clara said. "More people to watch me tremble."

"You will not be trembling by then," Harper said confidently. "At least, not more than the rest of us. And if a mysterious rider shows up, we will just out-ride them."

"Is that your plan?" Clara asked.

"Obviously." Harper tipped her chin up. "I am going to be legendary. People will tell stories of my diagonals for years."

Clara laughed again, and this time it did not feel forced. "I am pretty sure they already do."

They finished walking Aspen and took him back to his stall. Clara stripped off the saddle and pad, hanging them neatly on the rack. She ran a cool, damp sponge over Aspen's neck and chest, then brushed him until his coat glowed and his breathing had slowed.

When she finally stepped back, Aspen was relaxed, one hind leg cocked. He snuffled her jacket pockets hopefully.

"I do not have any treats," she said, then remembered the carrot in her bag. "Actually, that is a lie."

She retrieved the carrot and held it out. Aspen took it delicately, crunching with obvious pleasure. Orange flecks sprayed her hand. She wiped them on her breeches without thinking.

As she latched the stall door, she glanced down the aisle. At the far end, Hannah stood talking to someone Clara did not recognize, a woman in a neat jacket with a clipboard tucked against her hip. They were bent over a stack of papers spread across a tack trunk.

As she watched, the woman gestured toward a set of faded banners rolled up in the corner, then toward the arena doors. Hannah nodded, her face thoughtful and serious.

Harper followed Clara's gaze. "That must be the show secretary," she said. "Hannah said she was coming early to help plan. They are talking about repainting the jump standards and getting new flowers and stuff."

"New jumps," Clara murmured. The idea made her stomach flip again. New things to trust. New obstacles.

"Do not look so scared," Harper said. "New jumps are pretty. Think of the Instagram possibilities."

"Because that is what this sport is really about," Clara said.

"Obviously." Harper bumped her shoulder. "Come on. Help me with Oliver's stall and then we can go spy on the plans."

"I thought you were on stall duty alone," Clara said.

"Technically," Harper said. "But you owe me for emotional support."

Clara rolled her eyes, but she grabbed a fork anyway. The simple rhythm of mucking a stall, fork in, lift, shake, dump, soothed her nerves. The barn sounds blended into a low, familiar hum.

In the next stall, Zoey was talking loudly to someone on the phone about outfit options for the show. Words like "sponsor-friendly" and "photogenic" floated over the wall.

"I am telling you," Zoey said, "if this rumor is true and some big-name sponsor is coming, I cannot be caught dead in last season's show coat. It is a matter of principle."

Clara shot Harper a look. Harper mouthed the words Big sponsor, then raised her eyebrows.

Clara's heart did a small, uncertain skip. So the rumor was spreading. She did not know whether to hope it was true or not.

As they worked, a faint breeze drifted in from the open doors, carrying with it the sound of the creek running full and bright. The scent of damp earth mixed with the hay. Somewhere outside, one of the foals whinnied, a thin, high sound that made the mares call back in deeper tones.

Winter had held on for a long time. Snowbanks had lingered in stubborn piles. The memory of ice and fear and silence had seemed to fill every corner of her mind. But now, standing in the barn with sweat drying on her skin from a real ride, with the promise of a show on the horizon and the barn bustling with preparation, Clara could feel something else slipping in through the cracks.

Possibility.

She slid the last forkful of soiled shavings into the wheelbarrow and set the fork aside. Harper wiped her forehead with the back of her hand and leaned on the stall door, breathing hard.

"Look at us," Harper said. "Doing honest work."

"Do not tell Luke," Clara said. "He will expect it all the time."

They both looked down the aisle again. Hannah and the woman with the clipboard were walking toward the tack room now, talking in low voices. As they passed, Clara heard a few words.

"...bigger than last year..."

"...confirmed entries from out of county..."

"...that rider from the old circuit..."

The words stuck in her mind like burrs. That rider from the old circuit.

"Did you hear that?" she asked Harper.

"Only that I should have better ears," Harper said. "What did they say?"

"Something about a rider from the old circuit," Clara said slowly. "Do you think..."

She trailed off, not entirely sure what she thought. A flicker of memory rose: show grounds in another town, bright lights, and a girl with a smile that had been all teeth and no warmth.

Harper shrugged. "Could be anyone. There are lots of old circuits. Maybe it is someone amazing. Maybe it is someone awful. Either way, they have not met us yet."

Clara wanted to believe that. She wanted to believe that whoever walked into Willow Creek's show this spring would be stepping into her world now, not dragging her back into theirs.

"Come on," Harper said, pushing off the stall door. "Let us go look at the jump standards. I heard Hannah is thinking about repainting them in the barn colors. And I want a say in the flower choices."

"Since when do you care about flowers?" Clara asked, following her.

"Since I realized my horse jumps better when the jumps look nice," Harper said. "He is vain."

"You are projecting," Clara said.

They walked toward the arena doors together, their boots thudding on the worn boards. As they stepped outside, the warm breeze met them again, lifting the hair at their temples. The sunlight had climbed higher, brightening the field where the foals dozed in the pale grass. The creek's voice was louder now, rushing with melted snow.

Clara shaded her eyes with one hand and looked out over the valley. The hills seemed less daunting in the soft light. The barn behind her felt solid and alive. Aspen's soft whicker drifted from his stall, as if he was reminding her he was still there, waiting.

Spring had come to Willow Creek. The world was waking up.

And for the first time since the fall, Clara felt like she might be waking up with it.

2

By Friday, the barn smelled like paint, polish, and barely contained nerves.

Clara stood in the aisle with a brush in one hand and a dripping paint roller in the other, squinting at the jump standard in front of her. The rough wood had already soaked up the first coat of white, and she was working on the second, trying not to leave streaks. A drop of paint landed on her breeches, right on the knee.

"Great," she muttered. "Now I look like I lost a fight with a seagull."

Behind her, Harper laughed. "It is a good look for you. Artsy. On trend."

"You got more of it on yourself than the standard," Zoey observed from where she sat perched on an upturned bucket, scrolling on her phone. She had been assigned to "supervise" after she had almost backed into the fresh flower boxes and ruined a whole tray.

"At least I am doing something," Harper said. A streak of white ran through her braid like a misplaced highlight. "You are just sitting there making fun of us."

"I am researching," Zoey said without looking up. "Do you know how many sponsored riders have their own content channels now? It is a lot. And they all have really coordinated outfits. If this sponsor rumor is true, we have to be ready."

Clara tried not to think about sponsors. Or outfits. Or the fact that her show coat was three years old and had a little wear mark on the cuff where Aspen had chewed it once as a baby.

"Maybe we should focus on making the jumps not look like they belong in a haunted house first," Harper said. "Then we can worry about outfits."

"Speaking of," a voice called down the aisle, "how are my artists doing?"

Hannah walked into view, hands on her hips, her light brown hair pulled back into a practical ponytail. There was a smear of dirt on her cheek and a satisfied sparkle in her eyes, the look she got when barn projects were finally starting to look like something.

"We are transforming these standards into works of art," Harper said. "One drip at a time."

"I can see that," Hannah said, smiling. "They look good. Or they will, once you do the blue trim."

Clara glanced at the open cans near their feet. The barn colors, deep blue and crisp white, gleamed inside. It made the whole project feel more official somehow, like they were repainting not just wood and rails, but the way the barn presented itself to the outside world.

"Are we really getting new banners too?" Zoey asked, putting her phone away at last. "I heard a rumor about that."

Hannah's smile shifted into something more reserved. "We are looking into it," she said. "If things work out."

"If what works out?" Zoey pounced on the hesitation, all energy now. "Is it about the sponsor? Is it real or not? You have to tell us, it is cruel to keep secrets."

Hannah hesitated for a second longer, then sighed. "All right. Since it has clearly turned into the worst kept secret in the county."

Zoey and Harper exchanged a triumphant glance. Clara set down her roller without meaning to, her heart starting to beat faster.

"There is a possibility," Hannah said carefully, "that we will be partnering with a sponsor this season. It is not official yet. We have a visitor coming today to look at the facility and see if we are a good fit."

"Today?" Harper repeated. "As in today today?"

"Yes," Hannah said. "This afternoon. So I need everyone on their best behavior, which means no antics, no screaming across the arena, and definitely no riding bareback over the flower boxes like last time."

"That was one time," Harper said indignantly. "And it was Zoey's idea."

"It looked cool," Zoey added.

"It also almost flattened my begonias," Hannah said. "So no repeats. Understood?"

"Yes," they chorused, although Zoey's tone made it sound more like a suggestion than an agreement.

Clara swallowed. "Who is the sponsor?"

"His name is Victor Hale," Hannah said. "He runs Hale Performance Gear. They do saddles, bridles, show jackets, that sort of thing. He is very well connected in the show world. Having his support would be a big deal for Willow Creek."

Zoey's eyes lit up as if someone had switched on a marquee. "Performance gear? Like customized stuff? Are we talking embroidered saddle pads? Monogrammed jackets?"

"We are talking maybe," Hannah said firmly. "No promises. He is just coming to look around and watch a few rides. That is all. So please do not scare him away."

"Who is riding for him?" Harper asked.

Hannah hesitated again, and Clara's stomach clenched.

"He asked to see a couple of our riders who show regularly," Hannah said. "Luke and I made a list. Nothing is final, but he is definitely interested in seeing one of you on Aspen, Clara."

The paint roller slipped in Clara's hand and clattered onto the tarp. She scrambled to grab it before more paint splashed.

"Me?" she said, incredulous. "Why me?"

"Because you and Aspen have presence in the ring," Hannah said as if it were obvious. "You are a strong pair. You have done well at the shows you entered, even with the setback this winter. And, frankly, your story is compelling."

"My story," Clara repeated, and the words tasted odd. Like something being packaged.

"You came back from a fall," Hannah said gently. "You did not quit. Sponsors like riders who show grit and resilience. It reflects well on their brand."

Behind her, Harper muttered, "Told you your brand was terrified and awesome," and then coughed to cover it.

Clara's cheeks heated. She stared down at the half painted standard. The thought of some stranger watching her ride and judging her not just as a rider but as a walking advertisement made her stomach twist.

"I do not know if I am ready for that," she said quietly.

"You will not be doing anything you have not already done in a lesson," Hannah said. "Luke will be right there. We are not asking you to jump a meter thirty. Just ride the way you always do."

"That is the problem," Clara said. "The way I always do lately is nervous."

"You are better every day," Hannah replied. "Luke says your ride earlier this week was one of your strongest since the accident. If he did not think you could handle this, he would not have agreed."

Clara looked up sharply. "He agreed?"

"He did," Hannah said. "He is talking to Victor now about what to expect. They should be here in about an hour."

An hour. That was suddenly not a lot of time.

Zoey was practically vibrating. "What can we do to help? Should I redecorate the lounge? Should we make a welcome sign? Should we have a photoshoot?"

"Please do not," Hannah said. "What you can do is finish painting these standards and then groom your horses. If Mr. Hale wants to see more of the barn after the rides, I want everything looking clean and professional."

"Yes, ma'am," Harper said, saluting again with her paintbrush.

Hannah's expression softened. She looked at Clara. "You can say no," she added in a lower voice. "If this feels like too much, we will tell him you are not available. There are other riders."

The relief that rushed through Clara at the words surprised her. So she did have a choice. But underneath the relief, something stubborn stirred.

She thought of Aspen's steady ears in the arena, his willingness to try again even after he had slipped and scared himself. She thought of all the nights she had replayed the fall, wondering if she would ever feel like a real rider again, not a broken one.

If this Victor Hale person was the kind of sponsor who only wanted perfection, maybe he was exactly the kind of test she needed to face.

"I will do it," she heard herself say, before she could talk herself out of it.

Hannah gave a small, satisfied nod. "All right. Good. It will be a simple ride. Walk, trot, a little canter, a few small fences if you are comfortable. Show him who you and Aspen are."

"Who we are," Clara repeated, trying to imagine that as something strong rather than fragile.

As soon as Hannah walked away, Harper leaned over and bumped her shoulder. "Look at you," she said. "Being brave without even consulting me first."

"Maybe I am learning from the bad influence," Clara said faintly.

Zoey flopped back onto her bucket with a dramatic sigh. "I cannot believe you get to be the chosen one," she said. "Well, one of the chosen ones. Hannah said a couple riders. Still. A sponsor. This is huge."

"It is just a possibility," Clara said. "It is not like he is going to walk in and hand out contracts like candy."

"He might," Zoey said. "Have you seen the videos of other barns?

Sometimes sponsors basically live at the ring, taking pictures, giving away gear, doing interviews. They have their own tents at big shows."

"This is not a big show," Harper said. "It is Willow Creek's Spring Show. Relax."

"Big things can start small," Zoey said. "What if we are his new project? Imagine showing up at the next circuit with custom gear and a trainer who has connections. People would actually know who we are."

There was a longing in her voice that Clara recognized. It was the same thing that had tugged at her when she had first started showing. The idea that if she rode well enough, she could be more than just a girl on a horse, she could be someone.

"I am not even sure I want people to know who I am," Clara muttered.

"That is because you are humble," Zoey said. "It is not healthy."

"It is very healthy," Harper said. "Also, not everyone wants their riding turned into a brand. Some of us just want to jump things without dying inside."

Zoey sighed again, but she did not argue.

They finished the painting faster after that, working in focused silence. When the last standard was standing in a neat row to dry, gleaming white with crisp blue tops, Clara felt a small glow of pride. The arena was starting to look like a show ring.

By the time she had washed her hands, changed into clean breeches and a fitted polo, and brushed her hair into a low, neat ponytail, the nervous buzzing inside her had reached a full hum. She tried to burn some of it off by grooming Aspen extra thoroughly. His coat gleamed under the brush, and his mane lay in tidy, even sections.

"You look better than I do," she told him.

He blinked at her, unconcerned.

Luke appeared in the stall doorway as she was picking out Aspen's hooves. He wore a clean Willow Creek jacket and his dark hair was actually combed. That alone told her this visit was important.

"How are you holding up?" he asked.

"Like someone who is about to be judged on every tiny thing," she said. "So, you know. Great."

"That honest, huh?" He leaned one shoulder against the door-frame. "I talked to Hannah. She said she told you that you can opt out."

"I know," Clara said. "I want to do it. I think."

"You think," he repeated.

"I want to want to do it," she corrected. "Does that count?"

His mouth quirked. "It counts enough. We will keep this low key. Mr. Hale will watch from the rail. I will run the lesson like any other. If at any point you feel like it is too much, you say so and we stop. His opinion does not decide your worth as a rider."

She nodded, trying to let the words sink in past the noise in her head. "What is he like?"

Luke's expression changed slightly, his eyes narrowing just a fraction. "He is very polished," he said. "Knows what to say. Knows who to talk to. He has worked with some very big names."

"That sounds like a good thing," Clara said cautiously.

"It can be," Luke said. "He has helped some barns go from small local places to serious contenders on the circuit. But sponsorships like his come with expectations. Image, results, visibility. He is not doing this out of charity."

She swallowed. "Do you trust him?"

Luke was quiet for a moment. "I trust that he is very experienced at this game," he said finally. "I trust that he knows how to make things look good. I do not know yet if that is the same as being good for us."

"You do not really like him," she translated.

"I do not really know him," Luke corrected gently. "That is what today is for. For all of us. We see if Willow Creek feels right to him, and if he feels right to us."

Clara nodded again. Saying it that way made it feel less one sided. They were choosing too.

"Besides," Luke added, "he asked to see not just your riding, but how you relate to your horse. He says he values sensitivity and partnership. That is one of the reasons I agreed to let him watch you with Aspen."

The knot in her chest loosened a bit. "He did?"

"Yes. He saw some video from last year's show," Luke said. "The one where Aspen spooked at the banners but you talked him through the last line instead of just driving him at it. That apparently impressed him."

Clara remembered that round vividly. She had walked out feeling like she had barely held things together, yet when she had looked at the scoreboard they had still placed. She had not known anyone important was watching.

"Okay," she said. "Okay."

"Good." Luke tapped the door lightly. "He should be here any minute. Finish tacking up and meet us in the outdoor. The footing has finally dried out enough."

The outdoor arena. Clara's pulse jumped. The last time she had shown at Willow Creek, most of her classes had been indoors. The fall that had sidelined her had happened at another barn, on slick ground that had looked fine until it was not. She had not ridden a full course outside since then.

Aspen snorted and nudged her arm hard enough to rock her sideways.

"Fine," she told him. "I get it. You are ready. Stop yelling."

She finished tacking up with extra care, checking every strap twice. When she led Aspen out of the barn, the world felt too bright. The sun had slid westward, casting long shadows across the valley. The breeze had picked up just enough to lift the new banners that Hannah and the others had hung that morning along the fence. They fluttered gently in the light wind, blue and white, with the Willow Creek logo emblazoned on them.

At the far side of the arena, a man stood with Hannah and Luke.

She knew immediately that he had to be Victor Hale. No one else would look so completely at home and slightly out of place at the same time. He wore dark slacks and polished boots that had probably never seen real barn mud. His shirt was crisp white, open at the collar, with a tailored jacket over it that looked more corporate meeting than country stable. Pale sunglasses rested on his head, pushing back carefully styled dark hair that showed just a hint of gray at the temples.

Even at a distance, he radiated smooth confidence, like he was used to walking onto property and having everyone turn to look.

As Clara approached the arena gate, Harper appeared at her elbow as if she had been summoned by nervous energy.

"You okay?" Harper asked in a low voice.

"No," Clara said honestly. "But I am here."

"Good enough," Harper said, giving her a quick, fierce grin. "I will be on the rail. If he looks at you funny, I will throw dirt at him."

"Please do not throw dirt at the sponsor," Clara whispered, horrified and slightly amused.

"We will see," Harper said, then darted off to find a place by the fence.

Clara led Aspen through the gate. The footing had indeed dried, though it still had a darker color from the recent melt. The jumps they had painted stood in simple lines, rails gleaming against the sky. A few flower boxes, still empty, waited by the wings.

Luke stepped forward to take Aspen's reins while she mounted. She tried not to feel the glance that passed between him and Victor, a quick, measuring look.

"Mr. Hale," Hannah said, "this is Clara Bennett. She rides Aspen."

Victor Hale turned his full attention on her. His eyes were a clear, pale gray, sharp and weighing. Up close, the lines at the corners of his mouth looked more like they had been carved by practiced smiles than by laughter.

"It is a pleasure, Clara," he said, voice smooth as polished wood. "I have heard quite a bit about you."

"Nice to meet you," she said, her voice more breathless than she would have liked. She shifted her helmet under her arm, then remembered she should actually be wearing it and fumbled it onto her head.

He smiled, a flash of white teeth. "I watched some footage of you from last season," he said. "You have a lovely seat. Sensitive hands. This is Aspen?"

Clara nodded and patted Aspen's neck. "Yes. He is mine."

Victor stepped closer to study the gelding with an appraising eye. He reached out as if to touch Aspen's nose, then paused and let the horse lean in first, reading the reaction. Aspen sniffed his fingers and snorted softly.

"Good eye," Victor said, mostly to Luke and Hannah. "He has quality. Kind head. Intelligent eye. A little on the sensitive side, I would imagine."

"A little," Clara said. "He notices everything."

"That is not a flaw," Victor said. "In the right hands, it is an asset. Sensitivity can be shaped into brilliance. It is my philosophy that the best partnerships are made when both horse and rider think. That is what we look for in our sponsored pairs."

Our sponsored pairs. The phrase sat in the air between them, tantalizing and heavy.

"Why do you like Aspen for that?" Luke asked. His tone was neutral, but Clara could hear the question underneath: What exactly do you want from my rider and her horse.

Victor's smile did not waver. "As I said, I saw some of their rounds from last season. There was one in particular. The horse came into a line and hesitated at the second element. Many riders in her position would have pushed hard and forced the issue. She did not. She regrouped, talked him through it, rode the line with patience. They finished with small faults, but the partnership was clear."

Clara's cheeks burned. She remembered that moment as her

failure to be brave enough to kick on. She had sat quiet instead, coaxing Aspen over the second element like she was asking for a favor instead of giving an order.

"I value that kind of grit," Victor went on. "Not the artificial kind you get from empty bravado, but the steady kind that comes from knowing your partner and showing up anyway after things go wrong."

He looked at her as he said it, and something in his gaze made her feel transparent. Seen, and not necessarily in a bad way.

"Thank you," she said quietly.

"You had a fall this winter, did you not?" he asked, still in that mild tone, as if discussing the weather.

Her stomach clenched. "Yes."

"And you are back in the saddle already," he said. "That is the story, right there. Audiences respond to stories. Real ones. A rider who gets knocked down, gets up again, and keeps going. It is very compelling. I imagine it has not been easy."

"No," she said. "It has not."

"But you kept going," he said smoothly. "That is what matters."

Luke shifted his weight slightly. "Mr. Hale, Clara has been working very hard in her rehab. We are taking things step by step. Today, I want you to see a normal lesson, nothing staged."

"Of course," Victor said. "I would not want anything that is not authentic. That is not good for my brand or yours."

He stepped back, gesturing toward the mounting block. "Please, do not let me interrupt. I will observe quietly. Just pretend I am not here."

That, Clara thought, was impossible. His presence seemed to gather all the light and attention around him without him even trying.

She moved to the mounting block because there was nothing else to do. Her hands shook as she took the reins. Luke positioned Aspen calmly, one hand on the gelding's neck. As she swung her leg over and settled into the saddle, the familiar creak and shift grounded her, but the knowledge of eyes on her made every movement feel twice as large.

"Take your time," Luke said quietly, just for her. "Start with a walk. We will go through the same routine as Tuesday."

She nodded, throat too tight to answer. She squeezed her calves and Aspen stepped forward into a marching walk. The arena stretched out in front of her like a stage.

On the rail, Victor lifted a small notebook and began to jot notes, glancing between her and Aspen with that same calm focus.

They walked large around the arena, then on a circle. Luke kept his instructions simple. "Remember your breathing. Let your shoulders relax. Think of your legs wrapping around his barrel, not gripping."

As she turned down the long side, the new banners fluttered slightly. Aspen's ears pricked forward, but he did not shy. Clara softened her hands and talked to him under her breath.

"It is just fabric," she murmured. "You survived winter storms. You can survive this."

She could feel Victor watching, weighing not just her form but every small interaction. It made her want to ride perfectly, to give him nothing but clean lines and steady contact. It also made her hyper aware of every flaw.

They moved into trot. The first few strides were choppy, but she found the rhythm quickly. Luke had them change direction, do some circles, serpentines, transitions. Each time she wanted to stiffen, she heard his voice remind her of their exercises. Name what you feel. Stay here, not in the memory.

When Aspen stumbled slightly in a deeper patch of footing, her heart lurched. In the corner of her eye, she saw Victor's head lift, attention sharpening. She steadied her hands, gave with her hips, and rode him forward without overreacting.

"Good correction," Luke called. "You stayed centered. That is what keeps him balanced."

They added canter, just a few strides at first. The moment of lifting into the three beat gait still sent a bolt of fear through Clara, the echo of speed and loss of control. But Aspen's stride was contained and familiar, his ears flicking back as if asking, This? This is all?

"Nice," Luke said. "Keep your inside leg at the girth, outside leg a little behind. There you go. Do not worry about him. He will carry you. You just breathe."

When they came back to trot, Clara's arms felt like they had been carrying weights, even though she knew she had not been pulling. The tension of being watched was heavy.

"How are you feeling?" Luke asked softly when she passed near him.

"Like my heart is going to climb out of my throat," she said under her breath. "But I can keep going."

"Only if you want to," he reminded her.

She nodded once. "I do."

They took a short walk break. Victor consulted his notes, then looked up.

"Would you be comfortable with a small course?" he called. "Nothing big. Just a few fences. I would love to see how you and Aspen handle a line."

Luke glanced at Clara. She met his eyes. Her palms were damp inside her gloves.

"You choose," he said quietly. "We can stop here and I will explain why, or we can do a few crossrails. Either way, I have your back."

Clara looked ahead at the jumps they had painted. The white and blue rails looked bright but not intimidating, set at friendly heights. She thought of Aspen's eager trot, the way he had pricked his ears at the sight of the arena.

She did not want the first time she jumped in front of Victor Hale to be the last time she jumped for herself.

"Just the crossrails," she said. "Once around."

"All right," Luke said. "We will trot in, trot out. Keep your leg quiet, your eyes up. Focus on the rhythm. Aspen knows his job."

He lowered one of the verticals a hole, making it even smaller. Clara took another breath, wiped her glove subtly on her breeches, and picked up a trot again.

As she approached the first crossrail, the world narrowed. Hoofbeats, breathing, the feel of the reins. She counted quietly. One, two, one, two, one, two. At the base, she closed her leg. Aspen hopped over, neat and careful. She let her body fold, not jumping ahead, just following.

They trotted around to the second fence. It stood in the center, with two poles and a tiny box of fake flowers beneath. Aspen's ears flicked forward at the flowers, but he did not hesitate.

"Good," Luke called. "Now the line. Sit tall. Let him find his stride."

The line was short. Two low fences set five short strides apart. Nothing they had not done dozens of times indoors. The last time she had done a line outside, the ground had betrayed her. She shoved that thought aside.

Aspen locked on. She felt his muscles coil under her in anticipation. At the first fence, her body and his moved together, up and over. One stride, two, three, four, five, and then they were over the second.

It was not perfect. She felt herself collapse a little on landing, and her eyes flicked to the ground for a split second before she yanked them back up. But they did it.

"Again," Luke said. "Just once more, then we are done."

The second time, it was smoother. Her brain did not shout as loudly. By the time they came back to walk, her legs were trembling, but her mouth held a real, stunned smile.

"Excellent," Victor said from the rail. He clapped his hands together once, a brisk, decisive sound. "Very nice. You ride with feel. You do not override your horse. I like that."

"Thank you," Clara managed.

"You can walk him out," Luke said. "Let him stretch."

As she let Aspen stretch his neck and walk on a loose rein, Victor moved down the rail to fall into step alongside them on the outside. Hannah stayed near Luke, her expression thoughtful.

"I can see why Luke recommended you," Victor said conversationally. "You handle pressure well."

Clara almost laughed at that. If this was what handling pressure well looked like, she wondered what falling apart would have been. But he did not seem to be making fun of her. He meant it.

"I was very nervous," she admitted.

"As you should be," he said. "Only fools are never nervous. The trick is how you ride anyway. You breathed, you corrected, you did not let one mistake ruin the rest of the ride. That is exactly what we look for in a sponsored rider."

The words hung there. Sponsored rider. Her heart thumped.

"What does that mean, exactly?" she asked. "To be a sponsored rider. What would you want me to do?"

It felt strange to ask, bold even, but she wanted to know. This was not just something happening to her. She had a right to understand.

He smiled again, but this time there was something sharper behind it. "Good question," he said. "Many young riders get stars in their eyes and say yes to anything without asking. That usually ends badly."

He adjusted his jacket, then ticked points off on his fingers as he spoke. "If we decided to partner with Willow Creek, and with you, it would involve several things. First, equipment. We would supply you with our saddles, bridles, show pads, and jackets, free of charge. You would wear them at shows and in official appearances."

Official appearances. The phrase sounded like something celebrities did, not girls who still had to clean stalls on weekends.

"Second," he went on, "promotion. We would feature you and the barn in our campaigns. Social media, website, possibly print for certain markets. That means interviews, photoshoots, that sort of thing."

Clara's cheeks warmed. She thought of Zoey, who would probably faint from happiness at the idea of photoshoots. For Clara, the idea was more confusing than appealing. She liked photos of Aspen. Photos of herself, not so much.

"Third," Victor said, "visibility at shows. We would encourage you to enter a certain number of competitions each season. We might request that you prioritize particular events where our brand has a presence. In return, we would help cover some of your entry fees and travel costs."

That part was undeniably tempting. Shows were expensive. She had heard her mother quietly worry over budgets more than once. Having someone help pay for classes could open doors they could not otherwise afford.

"What about training?" Luke asked, stepping closer to the rail. His voice was courteous but there was steel underneath. "Would you expect to influence that as well?"

Victor considered him for a beat. "Our main interest is in results and representation," he said. "How you get there is largely up to you as the head trainer. Of course, we have certain guidelines. We like to see riders working with coaches who are known in the circuit, who attend certain clinics and events. We have relationships with several excellent professionals."

Clara's stomach tightened. "Would that mean changing barns?" she blurted.

"Oh, no," Victor said quickly. "If we sponsor Willow Creek, the barn itself becomes part of the partnership. We would not ask you to leave. However, we might occasionally ask you to ride in a clinic at another facility, or to attend a training week somewhere else. Perhaps at one of the larger centers we support."

"Like where?" Luke asked evenly.

Victor smiled, warming into his favorite subject. "You have probably heard of Knightfall Equestrian Center," he said. "They have been making waves on the circuit. Young blood, ambitious program. We have started working with them recently. They are up and coming competitors in this region. Very media savvy. They understand the modern game."

Clara had heard the name. Knightfall. It had come up in conversations at the feed store, in articles shared online. Big barn. Big money. Young riders who seemed to step fully formed into high classes with expensive horses and flawless outfits.

"They run excellent clinics," Victor continued. "We often encourage our riders to cross pollinate, as it were. Train in different programs. It raises everyone's level."

Luke's jaw tightened. It was a small shift, but Clara noticed. "We focus on horsemanship first here," he said. "Fancy programs come second."

"Of course," Victor said smoothly. "That is why I am here. A sponsor like me is only as strong as the barns and riders he supports. Authenticity matters. The audience can smell a fake a mile away. Willow Creek has a certain charm, a grounded feel. That has value. My job is to polish it, not erase it."

Polish it. The words slid over Clara's skin in a strange way. She thought of their freshly painted jumps, the banners, the idea of new gear with someone else's logo stamped on everything. She imagined herself in a glossy ad, smiling on Aspen's back with Hale Performance stitched across her chest.

Part of her wanted to reach for it. Another part worried about what would be left underneath once all that polishing was done.

"What about school?" she asked suddenly. "And family. I cannot just travel every weekend."

"Perfectly understandable," Victor said. "We work with parents and schedules. I am not talking about shipping you to Florida for three months. Not yet, anyway."

He laughed lightly. Clara tried to laugh too, but it came out weak.

"Any partnership would be spelled out clearly in a contract," he continued. "Expectations, obligations on both sides, compensation. No surprises. You would have time to read everything, discuss with your family and your trainer. I do not believe in trapping young riders in something they do not fully understand. That is bad business."

"Could we see an example?" Luke asked. "A sample contract. So we can understand what you usually require."

"Absolutely," Victor said. "I brought a packet."

He reached into the leather briefcase that sat on the arena bench behind him and pulled out a slim folder. He handed it to Hannah through the rail. She took it carefully, as if it were something fragile and valuable.

"In there," Victor said, "you will find our standard sponsorship terms. There is also a preliminary list of events we recommend for the season, based on the regional calendar. Some are local, some are a bit farther. And a list of other riders we are considering bringing under the Hale Performance umbrella. I like to think of it as forming a team."

A team. Clara tried to picture herself as part of a curated group of riders under the same brand. It felt flattering. Important. It also felt like stepping into something she did not fully control.

Hannah glanced at the top page as she tucked the folder under her arm. Clara caught a glimpse of dense text and bullet points. Near the back, there was a page with a table. Names, barns, locations. She thought she saw the phrase "Out of town show entries" at the top of one section before it was out of sight.

"As you can see," Victor was saying, "we would expect our partner barns to attend certain key events. You already host one, which is excellent. For the Spring Show, for instance, we have interest from several out of town riders. I have been encouraging some of our contacts to put your show on their calendar."

"Out of town riders," Hannah repeated. "From where?"

"A few neighboring counties," Victor said. "And beyond. Some from the old medal circuit. One or two from my other partner barns. I believe one of the names on the list will be familiar to you, actually. Megan Ward. She is looking to reinvigorate her season, and I suggested she might enjoy a fresh venue."

The name struck Clara like a stone dropped into a still pond. The ripples of old feelings spread through her chest. Megan Ward. The girl with the sharp smile and sharper tongue. The one who had spread whispers about her after a bad round last year, who had laughed in the warm up when Aspen spooked and called him "that broken baby."

Her fingers tightened on the reins. Aspen tossed his head slightly, feeling the change.

"You know her," Victor observed, faint amusement in his voice. "Excellent. Rivalries can be very engaging. Fans love a good story. Of course, on the ground, I expect sportsmanship. But from a narrative standpoint, prior history adds interest. Our media team can work with that."

Media team. Narrative. Fans. The words swirled in Clara's head. These were not just shows anymore. They were stories being packaged and sold.

She swallowed. "She is… talented," she said carefully. That part was true. Megan could ride. She also knew exactly how to dig under someone's skin.

"I hope you are not intimidated," Victor said lightly. "Competing against riders of her level is how you grow. And I suspect she will not be the only ambitious one at your Spring Show. With the right support, Willow Creek could become a real stop on the map. Not just a pretty valley with a nice little barn."

Nice little barn. She felt Hannah bristle beside Luke, but the barn owner's smile stayed politely in place.

"We like our valley," Hannah said. "And our barn. Growth is good, but not at the expense of who we are."

"Of course," Victor said again, that same easy agreement. "That is what I am proposing. An opportunity for both of us to grow in a way that benefits everyone. It is a partnership, not a takeover."

He turned his attention back to Clara and smiled. "You have given me a lot to think about today. I will be honest with you, Clara. A rider like you, with your story and your connection to your horse, is exactly the type of athlete we want front and center. With the right guidance, you could go far.”

She felt the compliment land, heavy with promise and pressure. “Thank you,” she said softly.

“Read the packet,” Victor said to Hannah and Luke. “Talk it over. I will be at a show in the next county tomorrow, then flying out for a week, but I will be in touch. If all goes well, I should have more concrete proposals by the time your Spring Show rolls around.”

He checked his expensive looking watch, then slipped his sunglasses back over his eyes. “I will take a quick tour of the rest of the facility, then I should be going.”

Hannah nodded and started to lead him toward the barn. As they walked away, Clara heard him say, “Your indoor could use a little updating, but the bones are good. And these views, well, you cannot buy that. Imagine a Hale Performance banner right there by the creek…”

Luke stayed by the rail until they disappeared around the corner, then let out a breath she had not realized he had been holding.

He stepped into the arena and joined Clara as she walked Aspen on a loose rein.

“How do you feel?” he asked quietly.

She thought about it. Her legs were still shaking a little. Her chest felt tight. Her head buzzed with words like sponsorship and media and rival. But under all of that, there was a small, steady flame.

“I did it,” she said. “I rode in front of him and I did not fall apart.”

“You did more than not fall apart,” Luke said. “You rode your horse, not your nerves. That is what matters.”

“He said my story was compelling,” she said. “Like I am a book he can sell. He even talked about Megan, like we are characters in some show he is planning.”

Luke’s jaw tightened again. “That is how people like him think,” he said. “Stories sell. Drama sells. It does not mean your experience is any less real. It just means you have to be careful about who controls the narrative.”

"Who controls it now?" she asked.

"You do," he said simply. "At least as far as your riding goes. You decide why you get on the horse, what you are riding for. Sponsors, ribbons, applause, those things can come and go. They can be good tools. They can also be traps if you let them become the main thing."

She nodded slowly. "What do you think of him? Really."

Luke was quiet for a long moment, watching Aspen's ears twitch as the gelding listened to their voices.

"I think he is very good at what he does," he said finally. "I think he sees you as both a rider and a product, and he does not see much difference between those things. That can be dangerous if we are not clear about our own boundaries."

"Do we have to say yes?" she asked. "If he offers."

"No," Luke said firmly. "We do not have to do anything. This is an opportunity, not a requirement. We will read the packet, talk it over. Your mom will need to be part of the conversation too. If at any point this feels wrong, we walk away."

"But it could help the barn," she said. "New gear, more shows, out of town riders coming in. I heard him say Knightfall is already working with him. If they get that advantage and we do not..."

She trailed off. The old competitive instinct stirred, the one that hated the idea of always playing catch up.

"Knightfall has their path," Luke said. "We have ours. Do not get caught in comparing everything. That way lies misery. What matters is whether this fits our values and your mental health. No sponsorship is worth breaking that."

His voice was gentle but unyielding. It made something in her unclench.

"Okay," she said. "We will think about it."

He nodded. "For now, cool out your horse. Give him a good groom. Maybe go watch the foals for a while. You did a big thing today. Let it sink in before you start worrying about the next thing."

She smiled faintly. "Is that your way of saying stop over-thinking?"

"Pretty much," he said.

She walked Aspen around the arena a few more times, letting the rhythm of his stride slowly smooth out the jagged edges of her thoughts. When she finally swung down and led him back to the barn, the sun had dipped lower, casting the valley in a warm, golden light.

Inside the barn, the atmosphere crackled with curiosity. Zoey appeared almost instantly at her side.

"How did it go?" Zoey demanded. "What did he say? Are we sponsored? Are we famous now?"

Harper came up behind her, eyebrows raised in silent question.

"We are not anything yet," Clara said, though her heart still pounded with the memory of Victor's assessing gaze. "He watched me ride. He said nice things. He gave Hannah a packet with a lot of words in it. He is thinking."

"And he said Knightfall is working with him," Harper added, having clearly eavesdropped on part of the conversation. "So now we have to decide if we want to join the fancy horse show club."

Zoey clasped her hands. "Yes. Yes we do."

Clara smiled, but it was a tired smile. As she unsaddled Aspen and rubbed the sweat marks from his coat, she let her mind drift back to the moment in the line, the feeling of trusting his stride and her own body.

No matter what Victor Hale decided, that feeling was hers.

Outside, the banners fluttered in the evening breeze. Somewhere, in a folder under Hannah's arm, names of out of town riders waited in neat rows, including one that made Clara's chest tighten.

Megan Ward.

And in some other barn, maybe at Knightfall Equestrian Center itself, riders were hearing Victor Hale say their stories were compelling too.

The Spring Show at Willow Creek was no longer just a local event. It was becoming part of something bigger, whether they were ready or not.

Clara rested her forehead against Aspen's neck for a moment, breathing in the clean, warm scent of horse.

"Whatever happens," she whispered, "we do this for us first, okay?"

Aspen sighed, leaning into her as if in agreement.

Outside, the last light of day slid across the valley, catching on the painted rails and the curling creek and the distant fields. Opportunity had arrived at Willow Creek, smiling and polished and full of promises.

Tension came with it, quiet but undeniable, like a tuning string pulled just a little tighter, waiting to see which way the music would bend.

3

By the next week, the banners around the outdoor ring had become part of the landscape. The flutter of blue and white no longer made Aspen flinch. It made Clara's stomach knot instead.

"Let's go again," she said, circling back to the starting point.

Luke, standing at the center of the arena with his hands in his jacket pockets, glanced at his watch. "We just did that grid twice," he said. "Walk break."

"I'm not tired," Clara said too quickly. "He isn't either."

Aspen's ears flicked back as if he disagreed. His neck was damp with sweat, dark patches showing under the saddle pad.

Luke's eyes narrowed just a little. "Warm up, grid, course, cool out. That was the plan."

"That was before we knew about the sponsor," Clara said, guiding Aspen into a tighter circle to keep him moving. "He said he wants to see results. If we are going to be ready for the Spring Show, we need to push."

"We need to build," Luke corrected. "Not burn out. Trot poles on a twenty meter circle. Then walk."

Clara pressed her lips together. She turned Aspen toward the line of ground poles anyway. His trot felt heavier than it had earlier, but she told herself that was because she was overthinking it.

One, two, three, four, over. His hooves tapped the poles with small knocks. He had been landing cleanly an hour ago. Now he clipped the last one again, the sound sharp in the quiet.

"See?" she muttered. "We are sloppy."

"That is not what that means," Luke said. His voice stayed calm, but she could feel his patience thinning. "He is tired. You are tired. That is all."

She ignored him and steered Aspen back to the little course. It was not even big. A crossrail, a vertical, the grid of three bounces they had been working on all week. Pony height, really. Nothing like the fences she used to dream about.

"Clara," Luke said, warning in his tone now.

"Just once more," she insisted. "Please."

He exhaled. "Once. Then we walk. If you do not listen to me, the ride is over."

She swallowed and nodded. That was the last thing she wanted, to be told to dismount like a beginner who could not be trusted with her own decisions. She gathered up her reins and closed her legs.

Aspen surged into a canter, obedient as always, but there was a faint sluggishness to his stride now. She pushed him forward more than she should have, chasing the feeling of power she remembered from before winter, before the fall, before every ride had been wrapped in caution.

"Eyes up," Luke called. "Ride the rhythm, not the speed."

She tried. She really did. But somewhere between the second fence and the grid, the old panic sneaked in. Her heart started thudding too fast. Her hands tightened.

Aspen felt it.

He hesitated for a fraction of a second at the first pole of the bounce. His hind foot slipped in a patch of slightly looser footing, just a tiny skid no worse than a scuff in sand.

To Clara, it felt like the whole world dropped.

The memory slammed into her body so hard she forgot to breathe. Hooves sliding on icy ground. The sick lurch of losing balance. The weight of twelve hundred pounds tilting sideways.

Her vision tunneled. For one terrifying instant she was not in the safe, dry Willow Creek arena anymore. She was back on that other course, watching the horse in front of her go down, hearing people shout.

She yanked back on the reins without meaning to.

Aspen scrambled, trying to regain his balance and understand the conflicting signals. Somehow, he still popped through the grid, chest brushing a rail that clattered loudly to the ground.

"Whoa," Clara gasped, hauling him to a messy halt on the far side.

She was shaking. She could not stop. Her legs felt like jelly. Her hands were ice on the leather.

Luke was already striding toward them. "Breathe," he said, voice firm.

She sucked in a jagged breath. It caught halfway down.

"Again," he said. "Slow. In. Out."

She focused on his voice instead of the roaring in her ears. In for two counts, out for two. Her shoulders dropped an inch.

Aspen blew out a long breath, as if he had been holding his own.

"I am sorry," she whispered, leaning forward to rest a hand on his neck. He trembled under her palm, a fine, quivering line from withers to tail.

"It is okay," she said, though she did not know if she was talking to him or herself. "You did nothing wrong."

Luke picked up the fallen rail and slid it back into the cups with a soft clunk. Then he stepped to Aspen's head and laid a hand on the gelding's cheek, speaking quietly.

"He is fine," Luke said after a moment. "No harm done. You, on the other hand, look like you have run ten miles."

"I overreacted," Clara muttered, furious with herself. "It was just a little slip. It was nothing. I made it a big deal."

"It was something to you," Luke said. "Your brain remembered danger. That is not drama. That is trauma doing what it is wired to do."

"It has been months," she said, shame crawling up her throat. "I should be over it by now."

"There is no 'should' here," he said. "Healing is not a schedule you can cram for. It is not a test you can pass by studying all night."

His words only made the pressure in her chest worse. If she could not fix this by working harder, what could she do?

"Walk," he said. "Loose rein. Let him stretch."

She chewed on the inside of her cheek but let the reins slip through her fingers. Aspen's head lowered gratefully. His stride lengthened as the tension leaked out of his muscles.

They walked a full circuit in silence before Luke spoke again.

"What are you chasing?" he asked quietly. "Because it is not better riding."

"I am trying to be ready," she said. "For the show. For Victor Hale. Everyone is counting on this sponsorship."

"Everyone?" Luke asked. "Or just a few loud voices?"

She thought of Zoey talking about coordinated outfits, of boarders whispering about prize money, of Hannah looking at the old, cracked jump standards before they repainted them. The barn did need help. That part was true.

"Willow Creek could change," she said. "If this works. New gear. More shows. Maybe better footing someday. I cannot be the reason we lose that."

"You are not responsible for the fate of the entire barn," Luke said. "That is not on your shoulders."

"Victor Hale liked me," she insisted. "He said I was the kind of rider his brand wants. What if I mess it up? What if I choke at the show and he decides we are not good enough after all?"

Luke sighed softly. He walked beside them, keeping pace with

Aspen's plodding walk. "Clara, listen to me. You do not have to prove anything to anyone."

She stared straight ahead at the far fence. The banners there fluttered lazily in the breeze.

"It doesn't feel like that," she whispered.

"I know," he said. "Because right now you are letting one man with a shiny logo take up more space in your head than your horse, your own instincts, and your love for riding combined."

When she did not answer, he continued, "You are working hard. That is good. But there is a difference between working hard and punishing yourself. Between training and trying to erase fear by brute force."

She swallowed. "If I just ride more, maybe it will get easier."

"It will get easier," he agreed. "But not because you grind yourself into the ground. It gets easier because you stack small, positive experiences. You listen when your body says 'enough' instead of telling it to shut up. You build trust. With Aspen. With yourself."

She let his words turn over slowly in her mind.

"He expects a lot," she said after a moment. "Victor. You heard him. He has plans. Media. Results. A team. If I mess up, I am not just disappointing myself. I am making Willow Creek look bad."

"Victor Hale is one possible chapter," Luke said. "He is not the whole book. If we do end up working with him, it will be on our terms. Not at the cost of your health."

"What if he walks away?" she asked.

"Then he was not the right fit," Luke said, simple as that.

She wanted to believe him. She wanted to trust that walking away from an opportunity would not mean walking away from her dreams.

On the far side of the arena, a car pulled into the gravel lot. The sound of tires on stones drifted over the fence. Clara glanced over in time to see a sleek black SUV roll to a stop next to the older, mud-splattered trucks.

The doors opened. Three teenagers climbed out, their jackets matched in navy blue with silver piping. A stylized K was embroidered over the chest of each, along with a horse head logo she recognized from social media.

Knightfall Equestrian Center.

"Great," she muttered.

Luke followed her gaze. His expression did not change, but his shoulders stiffened.

"I forgot they were coming today," he said. "Schooling day. Hannah set it up last month. Before all the sponsorship talk."

"Those are Knightfall riders," Clara said. "Right?"

"Some of their junior team," he said. "Here to use the outdoors and get used to different jumps. It is good for our riders too. You can watch and see how they ride courses. Learn something, maybe."

She watched one of the new arrivals swing a saddle out of the back of the SUV with practiced ease. The rider was a boy about her age, tall and lean, with light brown hair that fell into his eyes when he laughed. He tossed a comment over his shoulder to the girl next to him, and she rolled her eyes, but she was smiling.

Clara recognized him suddenly from a photo she had seen online. Knightfall had posted it after a medal final last fall.

"That is Liam Carter," she said.

"You know him?" Luke asked.

"Not like know him know him," she said quickly. "Just from videos. He rides that black gelding, Knight's Honor. They won the junior medal at Silver Ridge."

Luke nodded. "He rides well. So do most of them. They train hard. They also have a lot of advantages you do not. Try not to compare."

Too late, she thought.

She watched the Knightfall riders head into the barn, their matching jackets neat, their tack immaculate. Even from a distance they looked like a unit, a tiny team moving in sync.

"What are they doing here?" she asked, knowing it made her sound territorial and hating that she felt it anyway.

"Same thing you are doing," Luke said. "Trying to get better. Different barn, same sport."

"Do you think Victor will sponsor them too?" she asked.

"He already does," Luke said. "Or their barn, at least. He told us that. He thinks of you as potential teammates, not enemies."

That did not make her feel better. It made her feel like someone had put her on a scale against people she had never even met.

"Okay," Luke said. "Enough brooding. You are spinning yourself into knots."

"I am not brooding," she said.

"You are absolutely brooding," he said. "Walk your horse. Then we are done for today. No more grids. No more 'just one more time.'"

She wanted to argue. Instead, she slumped a little in the saddle, exhausted. Now that the adrenaline spike had faded, she felt wrung out. Her legs ached. Her back twinged where old bruises sometimes still complained.

"Fine," she muttered. "We walk."

They did. Around and around the arena, the new Knightfall car glinting in the corner of her vision. After a while, she focused on little things to keep her mind from spiraling. The creak of leather. The steady swing of Aspen's tail. The way his ears relaxed when she scratched his withers.

By the time she dismounted at the gate, the Knightfall riders were leading their horses toward the smaller warm up ring. One of them, a girl with a dark braid and sharp eyes, glanced over as Clara slid to the ground. Their gazes met for a heartbeat.

The girl's expression gave nothing away. Not friendliness, not hostility. Just assessment, the way she might look at another horse in the paddock. Then she turned and walked on, her navy jacket catching the light.

"Who is that?" Clara asked quietly.

"Not sure," Luke said. "Knightfall sends different kids to different schooling days. You will probably see more of them if they decide they like it here."

Great, Clara thought. As if she needed an audience for her internal meltdown.

In the barn, the air hummed with a new mix of sounds. Knightfall riders talking to Willow Creek boarders, tack clinking, the slightly different rhythm of unfamiliar horses walking on concrete.

Harper appeared the moment Clara led Aspen into the aisle. She took one look at Clara's face and dropped her joking tone.

"What happened?" Harper asked. "You look like you saw a ghost."

"More like relived one," Clara said softly, unclipping Aspen's girth with fingers that still shook a little. "He slipped. Just a tiny bit. I freaked out."

"Oh," Harper said. Her expression turned serious. "I am sorry."

"It was nothing," Clara said quickly. "I made it into something huge. I was pushing too hard. Luke said I am trying to prove things that do not need proving."

"Sounds like something he would say," Harper said. "Was he right?"

Clara hesitated. "Maybe."

"Probably," Harper said, reaching to help slide the saddle off Aspen's back. "He usually is. Annoying, but true."

Behind them, a new voice floated down the aisle. "Do you know which arena we are using first?" It sounded confident, practiced.

Harper glanced over Clara's shoulder. "Guests," she murmured. "Knightfall has landed."

Clara turned her head slightly. Liam Carter was there, closer now, leading a sleek black gelding whose coat shone like it had been polished for hours. The horse's name was stitched in silver on his halter.

Knight's Honor.

Liam's gaze flicked over Clara, Harper, Aspen, the tidy but older barn. He smiled politely. "Hey," he said. "We are from Knightfall. Coach Amber said we could school here today?"

"Yeah," Harper said. "Outdoor and lower arena. I think Hannah was going to set some lines for you."

"Cool," Liam said. His eyes lingered on Aspen for a second. "Nice horse."

"Thanks," Clara said automatically.

He nodded once, then moved on, calling something to the girl with the dark braid behind him. She rolled her eyes and said something that made him laugh.

Harper watched them go. "Well," she said. "They seem... intense."

"They seem like they know exactly what they are doing," Clara said. "And exactly where they are going."

Harper nudged her. "So do you," she said. "Even if you forget sometimes."

Clara was not sure that was true. More and more, it felt like the path in front of her was splitting into shiny, unfamiliar directions. Sponsor. No sponsor. Local shows. Bigger circuits. Barns like Willow Creek. Barns like Knightfall.

All she had wanted, once, was to ride. To jump. To feel the arc of a good fence and the solid landing on the other side.

Now, every jump felt like a test she could fail for someone she had never met.

She ran the soft brush over Aspen's neck in slow, steady strokes, trying to find the quiet inside his breathing again.

"You don't have to prove anything to anyone," Luke had said.

Maybe that could be true. Someday.

Right now, with Knightfall riders in the ring and Victor Hale's words in her head and whispers about out of town competitors floating through the barn, it did not feel true at all.

Outside, the sound of hooves picked up as the Knightfall horses trotted into the lower arena. Voices called out fence numbers and distances. It was training, same as any other day.

Inside Clara's chest, the pressure kept building, one careful, perfect stride at a time.

4

The Spring Show grounds were beginning to take shape. The new banners fluttered crisply along the fences, the repainted jumps gleamed under the morning light, and riders from different barns milled around the warm-up ring, stretching stiff winter legs and showing off new tack. The air almost hummed with the mixture of nerves and anticipation.

Clara tried to focus on grooming Aspen, brushing long strokes down his shoulder until the dust lifted and his coat shone. She told herself it was just another schooling day before the show. Nothing special. Nothing to dread.

But something heavy sat in her stomach. A weight she couldn't shake.

The barn door slid open behind her, letting in a burst of chilly air and the sound of a trailer ramp hitting gravel. Clara didn't look up at first. Trailers came and went all week. Visiting riders. Knightfall's juniors. Local boarders getting in extra practice.

But a voice floated down the aisle—bright, sweet, and edged with something metallic.

"Well, well. If it isn't Clara Bennett."

Clara froze, the brush pausing mid-stroke. Slowly, she turned.

Megan Ward walked toward her like she owned the barn.

Her glossy dark braid swung neatly over one shoulder. Her jacket —expensive and perfectly fitted—looked like it had stepped out of a catalog shoot. And behind her, stepping off the trailer with a proud arch of his neck, came Evermore.

The bay gelding's coat gleamed almost wet in the light, his mane neatly pulled, his tail wrapped. His hooves landed with sharp confidence on the concrete. But when he shifted sideways, Clara caught a flicker of something odd—a half-stumble, a hesitation in his left hind before he squared up again.

A flaw so small Clara might have imagined it.

She didn't have time to think more because Megan was already reaching her.

"Oh, Clara." Megan clasped her hands together in a picture-perfect gesture of surprise. "I had no idea you were still riding."

Still riding. As if the accident had ended her career. As if getting back in the saddle had been some remarkable, against-the-odds feat Megan hadn't expected her capable of.

Clara forced a breath. "Hi, Megan. I didn't know you were coming to this show."

"Oh, totally last-minute decision," Megan said breezily. "Victor mentioned the event, and I thought... why not? New year, new venues." She glanced around the barn aisle as if assessing the place. "It's cute here."

Cute. Like Willow Creek was a quirky little hobby barn instead of the heart of their valley.

Aspen shifted closer to Clara, sensing the change in her posture. His ears flattened a degree—not pinned, but wary. Clara laid a hand against his warm neck, anchoring herself.

"You remember Aspen," Clara said, because doing nothing felt worse. "He's doing well."

"Yes, he looks... spirited." Megan took a small step back, just enough to convey judgment. "But that's good for you, right? Keeps things exciting. Especially after everything that happened last winter."

The accident wasn't mentioned by name—but Clara felt it all the same. Like someone dropping ice cubes into her shirt.

She forced her jaw to unclench. "He's fine. We're both fine."

"Of course you are," Megan said with a syrupy smile. "Some riders just don't bounce back. But you... you're clearly doing your best."

Doing your best. Code for struggling. Code for "You're still broken, aren't you?"

Clara opened her mouth to respond, but movement at the arena gate caught Megan's attention. Victor Hale stood there, speaking with Hannah as the two observed the schooling riders. He looked just as polished as the day he visited, sunglasses pushed back into his dark hair, expression unreadable and confident.

"Oh!" Megan's smile sharpened. "There he is. Victor hasn't seen Evermore go in months. He's going to be thrilled."

Clara's stomach flipped. "You know him well?"

"Of course." Megan's laugh was light and practiced. "He's been advising me on my season. We've talked a lot about which shows will make the biggest splash. He's so supportive. He really cares about where this sport is going."

Translation: he cares about riders who look impressive on paper.

Before Clara could decide what to say, Megan leaned in slightly. "He was surprised, you know. When he heard you'd had a fall. He said he remembered you being such a steady little competitor." She paused, then sighed as if pained. "Trauma can really change a rider."

Clara felt the words like tiny pins against her ribs.

Aspen's head rose higher, tension moving into his body like he was absorbing hers.

"Megan," Clara said quietly, "I'm not interested in comparing stories."

"Oh, sweetie." Megan tilted her head sympathetically. "It's not a comparison. I just think it's brave that you showed up. Especially knowing how competitive this season is going to be." Her voice lowered, soft as velvet. "There's going to be a lot of pressure."

Clara didn't have to ask what she meant.

Pressure to look good for Victor.

Pressure to compete against Megan.

Pressure not to fall apart in front of everyone.

"Anyway." Megan flashed a dazzling smile. "I should get Evermore ready. He needs a careful warm-up today. He's feeling… special."

As she turned, Clara saw it again—a tiny irregularity in Evermore's step. Not constant. Not obvious. Just enough to plant worry like a seed.

"Did you see that?" Clara whispered to Aspen. "Or am I imagining things?"

Aspen flicked his tail, uncertain.

Before she could process it, Luke appeared beside her, wiping his hands on a rag.

"Everything all right?" he asked, scanning her face. He'd no doubt noticed the tension from halfway down the barn.

"That was Megan," Clara said unnecessarily.

"I saw." Luke's jaw tightened just slightly. He didn't need to say the rest. He remembered the rumors. The way Megan had smiled while telling people Clara's fall had been caused by "overconfidence." Or that Aspen was "too much horse for her."

"What did she say?" Luke asked.

"Nothing," Clara said. Then, because Luke could always see straight through her, she added, "Nothing important."

He didn't push. "You're carrying your shoulders around your ears again."

"I'm fine," she said automatically.

"Fine doesn't make your horse nervous," Luke said.

Clara blinked and looked at Aspen. His muscles were tighter beneath her hand. His nostrils had flared just enough to show worry.

Clara let out a shaky breath. "Sorry, boy." She stroked him gently. "It's just… Megan."

Luke nodded once. "Ignore her."

"She knows Victor," Clara said. "She's riding Evermore for him. She said she's part of his plans."

"She says a lot of things," Luke replied evenly. "Some true. Some for effect."

Clara hesitated. "Do you think Victor is… considering her too?"

Luke shrugged. "Probably. He's a businessman. He looks at all his options."

And Clara hated that his answer made her chest tighten again.

As they talked, Megan led Evermore into the indoor arena for his warm-up. The gelding's bay coat shone under the overhead lights. He arched his neck beautifully, every inch a show horse with presence.

Victor Hale drifted toward the viewing window, expression attentive. He watched Megan with the same measured, appraising interest he had shown Clara and Aspen.

But there was something different about the way he watched Megan.

Less curiosity. More calculation.

"Great," Clara muttered. "He likes her."

"He likes whatever looks good on camera," Luke said. "That's not the same as liking her."

Clara bit the inside of her cheek. "Do you think she'll compete in the junior classes? The same ones as me?"

"Probably," Luke said. "But you don't have to beat Megan to be successful."

"Feels like I do," Clara whispered. "Especially if Victor is watching both of us."

Luke turned fully to her. "Clara. Look at me."

She did.

"You are not in a contest to impress Victor Hale," he said. "You're a rider. A good one. And you ride for yourself and your horse first."

Clara nodded, but she didn't fully believe it.

Not when Megan Ward was practically spinning circles around her confidence.

They were interrupted by footsteps clicking down the aisle. Megan reappeared, cheeks flushed from her warm-up, braid swaying with each step.

She paused beside Clara again, eyes wide and falsely warm. "Oh! Before I forget—guess who I trained with last month? Liam Carter."

Clara stiffened. "From Knightfall?"

"Yes!" Megan clasped her hands dramatically. "He's amazing. Really sharp. Such a natural talent. His trainer says he's going to dominate the summer circuit." Her smile brightened dangerously. "He said I should enter all the same classes he's doing. Apparently, our riding styles complement each other."

Clara felt that same cold trickle down her spine. Megan wasn't just competing. She was building alliances—Knightfall riders, Victor Hale, momentum Clara couldn't match.

"That's great," Clara managed.

"Isn't it?" Megan beamed. "You'll see him around, I'm sure. He said he might come watch the Spring Show, depending on his schedule." She tilted her head. "Oh—and Victor mentioned he wants to compare riders across barns this season. Should be fun!"

With that final, sugary dagger, Megan flounced away, Evermore's hoofbeats tapping behind her.

Clara stood frozen for a moment.

Then she exhaled shakily.

"Okay," she whispered. "That... that's a lot."

Luke didn't sugarcoat his reply. "It is."

Aspen pressed his nose into her shoulder, seeking reassurance. Clara rested both hands against his cheek.

"I don't want her to get to me," she said quietly.

"Then don't let her," Luke replied. "Her confidence is built on being loud. Yours is built on being steady. Those are not the same thing."

Clara let those words settle.

In the indoor, Megan asked Evermore for a canter circle. His left hind faltered—just a little. Enough for Luke to murmur, "Watch that. Something's off."

Clara saw it too. A fraction late behind. A tightness. A hint.

She didn't say anything.

But she felt a prickle of dread for the show ahead.

And for whatever storm Megan's arrival was about to bring.

Because the rival wasn't just back in the ring.

She was back in Clara's head.

5

By Thursday afternoon, the Spring Show course stood fully set in the outdoor arena. Freshly painted rails gleamed like polished bones, flower boxes overflowed with bright silk blossoms, and the new oxer—deep blue with white stripes—stood at the far end like a quiet test waiting to unfold.

Clara tried not to stare at it. She focused instead on the small vertical at the start of the line. Something she had jumped dozens of times. Something easy.

Aspen snorted beneath her, ears flicking, eager to move. He felt good today—fresh, responsive, his winter coat nearly shed out. He should have been the easy part of this ride.

Her brain was the hard part.

"Whenever you're ready," Luke called from the center. He had a clipboard in one hand, a pen tucked behind his ear. "Warm-up felt solid. Let's put the line together."

Clara breathed out, shortened her reins, and asked Aspen for a canter. He lifted smoothly, but her shoulders were already tense. The memory of Megan's smug smile from earlier in the barn replayed itself like an unwanted echo.

Evermore looks sharp today.

Victor loves a confident rider.

Liam Carter says my form is improving fast.

Her jaw tightened. She focused on the line ahead—vertical, five strides, vertical.

Simple.

Routine.

She aimed for the first fence, counted her rhythm, and tried to ride the stride the way she always had.

But halfway down the line, a gust of wind rattled the new banners at the far fence. Aspen's ears flicked. Clara's heartbeat lurched. Her hands tightened a fraction too much.

Aspen hesitated.

Just a half-step. Just long enough to destroy the stride.

"Leg!" Luke called sharply.

Clara reacted late. Too late.

Aspen chipped in at the second vertical, got underneath the base, and stopped abruptly with a lurch that snapped Clara forward onto his neck.

She gasped, catching herself with both hands in his mane.

For a moment, the world shrank to the thud of her heart and the hot prickle of shame burning across her face.

She heard footsteps approaching before she saw the rider.

"Well," Megan Ward drawled from the rail, reins loose in one manicured hand. "That was... brave."

Clara's stomach dropped.

Megan leaned casually against the fence, Evermore standing behind her like a glossy statue. "You really need to keep your eyes up, Clara," she said lightly. "If you look at the ground, Aspen will think you're planning a nap."

Clara forced her expression into something neutral. "Thanks," she said, because she couldn't think of anything else that didn't sound defensive.

"Oh, don't thank me," Megan said sweetly. "I'm just trying to help. Victor's very invested in riders who finish courses, you know?" She flicked her hair back over her shoulder. "The brand values champions."

Clara sucked in a breath so sharp she felt it catch behind her ribs. Aspen shifted restlessly, picking up the tension like a live wire.

Before she could respond, Victor Hale himself strolled up behind Megan, hands in his pockets, expression polished as ever.

"I caught the tail end of that," he said, his voice warm, almost paternal. "No shame in a mistake, Clara. But we can't let hesitation rule your ride." He nodded toward Aspen. "He needs you to make decisions, not apologize for them."

"I wasn't—" Clara started, then bit her tongue.

Victor's smile stayed soft but his eyes didn't. "You have talent. Don't waste it by second-guessing. Champions rise to the moment. Remember that."

He nodded politely to Luke, then walked away, Megan gliding behind him like a satisfied shadow.

Clara's throat tightened so hard she had to look away—to Aspen's mane, the sky, anywhere but the retreating pair.

"Hey," Luke said gently, stepping closer. "Look at me."

She blinked hard, lashes wet. "That was awful."

"It was a mistake," Luke said. "Not a prophecy."

She took another breath, sharp and quick. "I can't mess up like that. Not with them watching."

"Clara," he said, his voice steady, "you're not riding for Victor Hale."

"It doesn't feel that way," she whispered.

Aspen shifted again, unsettled. His muscles felt tight under her leg.

Luke held up both hands in the universal slow-down gesture. "Let's reset. Walk for a minute. Give him a breather."

She nodded numbly and let Aspen stretch down at a walk. She tried to breathe with him, matching his rhythm like Luke had taught her. But her mind kept pulsing with the same frantic loop:

You choked.

You messed up an easy line.

He saw.

They saw.

Harper, watching from the rail, gave her a worried look, but Clara couldn't meet it.

When they finally picked up canter again, Clara tried to steady herself.

Vertical. Five strides. Vertical.

She repeated it like a mantra.

But as she circled toward the start, her gaze caught on the far oxer—the tricky one with the blue-and-white rails. Something about the bottom rail looked slightly crooked, off by a fraction of an inch.

"Luke," she said suddenly, her voice wavering, "that oxer... are the rails even?"

Luke squinted. "Hmm. Might be the footing settling. I'll have the jump crew check it later. Coach Amber Leigh trained some of them last month—good group, but not much show experience."

Amber Leigh. A name Clara recognized vaguely from articles about regional clinics—tough, brilliant, exacting. Someone Knight-fall riders trained with often.

Another reminder that this show wasn't small anymore.

Clara forced herself to focus on the line in front of her. She gave Aspen a soft cluck and cantered forward.

This time, she kept her eyes up.

This time, she added leg when she felt her hesitation.

This time, they made it through the line—still messy, still rattled—but without stopping.

As they landed, relief washed through Clara so suddenly it left her dizzy. She swallowed hard, trying to hold the rest of her emotions inside.

"Good correction," Luke called. "Now breathe."

She did.

Sort of.

But as she walked Aspen out, she felt the tremble in her hands. The ache behind her eyes. The pressure of everything she wasn't saying.

She didn't cry.

She wouldn't.

Not here.

Not with Megan riding perfect circles in the warm-up. Not with Victor Hale watching riders like a man picking stocks.

So she straightened her shoulders, patted Aspen's sweating neck, and whispered, "We got through it. That's something."

Aspen flicked his ears uncertainly, as if he wasn't quite convinced.

And Clara wasn't either.

Because cracks had formed—hairline fractures in her confidence.

Not yet enough to break her.

But enough that she could feel the fault lines shifting beneath her feet.

6

The day before the Spring Show felt less like a Friday and more like the inside of a shaken snow globe—everything swirling, glittering, unsettled.

Willow Creek Stables hummed with activity from dawn. Horses were bathed and braided. Tack gleamed with fresh polish. Riders buzzed through the aisles like caffeinated bees, each one either frantically preparing... or pretending not to be frantic at all. Someone had started the radio early, and upbeat pop music blended with the steady rhythm of sweeping brooms and clattering buckets.

Clara stood in the middle of it all, brushing Aspen's already-clean coat with long, methodical strokes. Her fingers moved automatically, but her thoughts darted everywhere at once.

"Do we have enough flower boxes?" Zoey asked from somewhere near the tack room.

"Only if you stop stealing them for your aesthetic shots," Harper replied.

"I am documenting the show preparations," Zoey said indignantly. "This is important content."

Clara didn't smile at their bickering like she usually did. Her stomach felt tight, knotted around the memory of yesterday's mistake. The chipped stride. Aspen's stop. Megan's condescending voice. Victor Hale's thinly veiled warning.

Champions rise to the moment.

Clara tried to shake the words out of her mind, but they stuck.

She finished brushing Aspen and moved to pick out his hooves. He shifted his weight toward her, nudging her gently with his shoulder. It was deliberate—his version of asking, *What is wrong? Why are you different today?*

Clara didn't answer him. She just ducked under the cross-tie and busied herself with his hind hoof.

The barn door banged open with a loud slap of wind, and two Knightfall riders stepped inside, their navy jackets unmistakable. They chatted quietly with Hannah, gesturing toward the outdoor arena.

"Is the scout coming today?" one of them asked, her voice carrying down the aisle.

"I really hope so," the other replied. "Coach Amber said he'd try to swing by. He's been looking for strong juniors for the medal qualifiers."

Scout. Medal qualifiers. The kind of whispers that sent a thrill through most ambitious young riders.

Clara felt her shoulders tighten.

Rumor had it Knightfall was pushing hard this season—new sponsors, new riders, new goals. If a scout really was coming to watch, they would certainly be looking at Knightfall's polished team.

And maybe... at whoever else Victor Hale had shown interest in.

Clara swallowed hard and pretended the hoof pick needed intense attention.

Aspen flicked an ear back, sensing her nerves like static.

"You're stiff as a board," Harper said, appearing in the aisle with a bucket of brushes. "Also, you're brushing him like he personally offended you."

"I'm fine," Clara said automatically.

"You've been saying that all morning," Harper pointed out.

"Because it's true."

"You're also clenching your jaw so hard I can hear it over the radio."

Clara ignored her and switched to Aspen's mane. She kept her strokes slow and controlled, trying to hide the tremor in her hands.

Down the aisle, Megan Ward arrived in a swirl of perfume and perfect posture. Evermore followed with a proud step—almost too proud. Clara instinctively watched his hind legs as he walked. The slight hesitation she'd spotted earlier week was still there. Subtle. Easy to miss.

Megan's trainer, a tall, crisp woman with silver-rimmed glasses, glanced at the gelding and nodded. "He looks perfect. Exactly what I want to see."

Clara blinked. Perfect? Evermore's stride wasn't perfect. It wasn't even normal.

But Megan smiled and tossed her braid. "Told you he's ready. He just needed time to settle. This footing is... quaint, but he can handle it."

Clara's hands tightened around Aspen's mane.

She knew better than to say anything—not her horse, not her business—but something in her chest prickled with unease. Ignoring a tiny lameness before a show? It was risky. Stupid. Dangerous for the horse.

She might have said something anyway... if Megan's next sentence hadn't knocked the breath out of her.

"Honestly, if anyone should be worried about footing, it's Clara," Megan said to her trainer with a tinkling laugh. "After the accident, she probably sees danger everywhere."

Clara flinched.

Her brush slipped from her fingers and hit the floor with a soft clunk.

The accident. She'd known it was coming. She'd known Megan

wouldn't be able to resist using it. But hearing the word whispered—
not as concern, but as gossip—hit her like a cold slap.

Harper stiffened beside her, eyes narrowing. "Ignore her," Harper
muttered. "She's threatened by you."

"She's not," Clara said quietly. "She's confident. And she knows
exactly what she's doing."

"That doesn't make her right," Harper said.

Clara didn't answer. Her throat was tight again, too tight.

She bent to pick up the brush, but Megan's trainer was already
striding past with Evermore, the gelding stepping proud and sharp
and just slightly... off.

Clara hesitated.

Should she say something?

Before she could decide, Luke's voice cut across the aisle.

"There you are. Good. We need a hand with the new jump."

Clara stiffened. "What new jump?"

"The one for tomorrow's Level Two Hunter class," he said. "The
builder dropped it off early. Come take a look."

She followed Luke to the outdoor ring, Aspen trailing behind in
his halter. The moment she saw it, her heart stopped.

The new jump towered near the far end—a wide oxer with a
carved wooden filler underneath. It wasn't high. Not yet. But the
design was tall, imposing, a wall of polished wood with a stylized
willow tree cut into the center.

"Wow," Harper breathed behind her. "It's... dramatic."

Luke nodded. "It'll be part of the show-jumping course tomorrow. Not for your division, Clara, don't panic. But they're testing it
today."

Clara's stomach didn't get the message. Her eyes tracked the
height, the spread, the way the wooden filler cast a long, sharp
shadow across the footing.

"It looks like something out of a championship," Zoey said,
walking up with a camera slung over her shoulder. "Shouldn't we get
a smaller version first?"

"It's fine," Luke said, though Clara noticed the faint crease in his brow. "It's solidly built, but it's different. Horses haven't seen it before. They'll look."

Clara swallowed. Aspen stood beside her, watching the jump with quiet curiosity, ears flicking between her and the obstacle. He nudged her shoulder again, gently but insistently.

"I know," she whispered to him. "I know."

Luke turned to her. "How are you feeling?"

"Fine," she lied quickly.

He raised an eyebrow. "You're breathing like you sprinted here."

"I'm just excited." She forced a smile. "Show energy."

"Uh-huh," Luke said slowly.

She kept her gaze on the jump, because looking at Luke felt too exposing.

Around them, riders moved in a constant flow. A few Knightfall juniors were schooling their horses nearby, their movements polished, precise. Clara overheard one of them say quietly:

"Coach Amber says the scout might stop by on his way home tonight."

Clara's pulse skipped.

Another replied, "I hope he sees my course. I want to make the list."

Clara stiffened.

There it was again. The sense that invisible judges were watching everything. That every stride, every breath, every tiny mistake mattered.

Pressure pressed over her like fog.

Luke must have seen her shoulders tighten because he gently touched her elbow. "Clara, hey. Look at me."

She did, reluctantly.

"You don't have to perform today," he said. "Not for me. Not for Megan. Not for Victor. Not for Knightfall."

Her throat tightened painfully. "Everyone keeps saying that. But it feels like everything I do is being measured."

"It's not."

"It feels like it."

Luke exhaled and looked out across the busy, buzzing barn. "I know. Show-eve nerves are real. But that's all this is. Nerves."

Clara wished she could believe him. She wished she didn't feel the whisper of panic climbing up her spine, triggered by a single overheard word—

The accident.

Clara wrapped her arms around Aspen's neck for a second, burying her face in his warm coat. He blew out a soft breath and leaned into her, steady as always.

"I'm okay," she whispered again.

It didn't feel true.

Not entirely.

When she straightened, she found Megan leaning against the fence, arms elegantly crossed, Evermore resting a hind leg beside her. Megan's lips curved into a small smile—almost invisible. Almost kind.

Almost.

Clara looked away quickly.

"I'm going to get Aspen settled," she said, grabbing the lead rope. "He needs a rest before dinner."

"You need one more," Luke said softly.

She didn't answer him.

Instead, she walked away with Aspen, letting her steps fall into a steady rhythm. But even as the barn lights glowed warmly around her and the evening breeze carried the scent of fresh shavings, Clara couldn't shake the feeling of being watched.

By competitors.

By scouts.

By a sponsor who saw her as part of a brand.

By a rival who saw her as a weakness.

She led Aspen to his stall and slipped off his halter. His eyes followed her as she backed away. When she turned, he reached over the stall door and nosed her shoulder again, almost stubbornly.

"I know," she murmured. "You're trying to help. I'm trying too."

A sharp whinny from outside made her jump. A Knightfall horse protested being clipped. Another rider laughed. The whole barn seemed louder, brighter, more chaotic.

She pressed a hand over her heart until it stopped racing.

Tomorrow would be the show.

And tonight... tonight she felt like she was standing on the edge of something bigger than anything she had prepared for.

Clara closed her eyes, breathed once, and whispered to herself:

"Just get through tomorrow."

But she wasn't sure she believed that either.

7

Morning arrived with a brightness that felt almost artificial, as if the sun itself understood that it was show day and had turned up the intensity accordingly. The valley glowed. The creek flashed silver beneath the footbridge. The grass gleamed with beads of dew that caught the light like scattered diamonds. Even the air felt sharper, pressed thin with excitement and nerves.

Willow Creek had been transformed overnight. Banners hung neatly along the fences, rippling in the breeze. The show office tent bustled with early arriving parents clutching coffee cups. The warm up arena rang with the sound of hoofbeats and clipped instructions. Riders zipped jackets, tightened girths, polished boots with frantic precision. It was the kind of morning that promised possibility and disaster in equal measure.

Clara stood beside Aspen's stall, her hands resting lightly on the gelding's cheek. His coat was brushed to a copper shine. His braids were tight and tidy. His eyes were soft, calm, steady. Everything she wished she could feel in herself.

"We can do this," she whispered. "Right?"

Aspen nudged her softly, pushing her back a step. A direct answer, if horses gave such things. He was ready. He wanted to move. He wanted to work.

Clara wished she could borrow his certainty.

Harper appeared in the aisle with a pair of spare gloves in one hand and an energy that bordered on chaotic flutter. "There you are. They just posted the order for your division. You are riding fourth."

"Fourth," Clara repeated. "That is soon."

"Soon is good," Harper said. "No long wait to overthink yourself. In and out. Like ripping off a bandage."

Clara thought of the oxer with the odd rail. The one that had unsettled her during schooling. The rails had been adjusted, but something about the jump still felt wrong. Too tall in appearance, too wide with the shadow of the wooden filler, too unfamiliar. She had not said as much aloud. Luke had already noticed her fear. She did not want to spell it out for him again.

"Luke wants you at the warm up ring in ten," Harper said. "You know he will have a plan. He always does."

Clara nodded, though her heartbeat thudded too fast to feel reassured.

Behind them, Megan breezed down the aisle with Evermore gleaming under a navy show sheet. The bay gelding stepped with such glossy pride that a few parents stopped to admire him. Megan soaked in every glance, smiling like the morning had been built just for her.

"Good luck," she called out to Clara in a sugary tone. "Fourth can be nerve wracking. At least you will get it over with."

Clara ignored the bait and lifted Aspen's bridle instead. Aspen leaned down to take the bit willingly, as if trying to help her stay grounded in simple things.

Girth. Saddle. Boots. Gloves.

One step at a time.

When they stepped out of the barn, the showgrounds stretched before them in full color. Riders trotted circles in the warm up ring, judges arranged papers at their table, and the smell of morning dust and freshly turned footing filled the air.

Luke waited at the mounting block, holding a crop and two small adjustment tools. His expression was calm. Focused. Exactly what Clara needed.

"You are early," he said as she approached.

"I did not want to rush," she said.

"That is good," he replied. "Deep breath. Today we ride the plan, not the worry. Understood"

She nodded.

"Mount up," he said.

She placed one foot in the stirrup, swung her leg over, and settled into the saddle. Aspen shifted beneath her, eager to move. Every sound around them seemed amplified. The crack of a rail in the warm up. A horse snorting. A woman laughing near the registration tent. The creak of leather under her own weight.

Luke stepped to her right side. "Walk around the warm up first. Let him stretch his neck. No circling thoughts. Stay with the horse."

She guided Aspen forward. The gelding moved with familiar rhythm, head lowering to loosen his muscles. His ears flicked toward her voice when she whispered small reminders.

"You are fine. I am here. You are fine."

Warm up riders passed on either side of her. A Knightfall junior popped over a vertical with perfect form. Someone's parent clapped loudly at a clean oxer. A volunteer adjusted a ground pole that had been kicked out of place.

Clara's mind kept drifting toward the main ring where the course waited behind white rails and flower boxes. She could see the oxer from here. Its dark wooden filler cast a long shadow across the bright morning footing. It was not even part of her division. Hers had a scaled down version. Yet her eyes kept going to the tall one, the original, the one that whispered of falls and misjudged strides and the memory she still carried.

Luke must have seen her staring. He appeared beside her again. "Eyes on your horse, not the jump."

She dragged her gaze back to Aspen's soft ears. "Sorry."

"You do not need to apologize," Luke said. "Just focus. Walk. Then we will trot. Then we will jump a small crossrail. Step by step."

He said it so simply that part of her unclenched.

She walked for five minutes, then picked up a trot. Aspen moved easily, stretching into the contact. She felt his barrel expand beneath her leg with every breath, steady and warm. When she asked for a canter, he lifted willingly, his stride smooth and controlled.

"Good," Luke said. "Keep that energy. You are riding, not surviving."

Surviving. The word made her stomach flip. She ignored it.

The first jump in warm up was a small crossrail. Clara guided Aspen toward it. He hopped over neatly, landing in a balanced canter. No hesitation. No uncertainty. Just training. Just partnership.

"Nice," Harper called from the rail. "That looked pretty."

Clara felt some of the tension melt from her shoulders.

Then she heard footsteps behind her. The sound of a camera clicking. She did not need to look to know who it was.

Victor Hale stood near the warm up gate with a sleek black camera in hand. His sunglasses were off. His eyes were fixed on her with calculating interest.

Every muscle in Clara's body tensed.

He raised the camera and took a photo the moment Aspen lifted into the canter.

No warning. No greeting.

Just documentation.

He wanted proof of how she rode under pressure.

Luke noticed and stepped into Victor's line of sight. "Warm up is not a photoshoot, Victor. Give the kids space."

Victor smiled a polite smile. "Of course. I am simply observing. No harm done."

Luke's jaw tightened, but Victor stepped back with a small nod, still too close for Clara's comfort.

Aspen felt the shift and shook his head. Clara stroked his neck and whispered to him until he settled.

Her warm up finished quickly after that. Luke gave her a final adjustment on her stirrup length, tapped the saddle lightly, and said, "You are ready."

Her heart pounded.

"Do not rush the gates," he added. "Ride like you do in lessons. Ride your horse. Trust your training."

Clara nodded, gripping the reins tightly.

The announcer crackled over the loudspeaker.

"Junior Hunters, Level One, please report to the in gate. First rider up in one minute."

That was not her. But it meant her division was on deck. Close enough that her breath caught.

Luke gave Aspen a final pat. "You will be fine. I promise."

Harper squeezed Clara's boot. "You are going to look amazing out there."

Clara smiled faintly. "I hope so."

The first rider went in. The crowd clapped politely at the end. The second rider finished with a small refusal. The third rider had a clean round.

Then the announcer said the words that made Clara's stomach drop.

"In the ring next, rider number seventy four, Clara Bennett on Aspen."

Her fingers tightened on the reins. She walked toward the gate. Aspen moved forward confidently, ears pricked. The sunlight made the rails inside the main arena glow with stark brightness.

When the gate steward nodded, Clara inhaled deeply, clucked to Aspen, and entered the show ring.

The jump crew stood along the edge, adjusting rails. The judge watched from the far booth. Parents lined the wooden fence, whispering comments.

Victor Hale stood near the back corner, camera ready.

And halfway up the stands sat someone Clara did not expect at all. A boy with light brown hair falling over his forehead. A notebook open in his lap. Pen tapping against his knee.

Liam Carter.

The boy from Knightfall.

He watched the ring with focused intensity. As if he were studying every rider. As if he were analyzing her in particular.

Clara swallowed hard. Her nerves spiked. But the bell rang to start the course, and she had no time left to think.

She steered Aspen toward the first fence.

A simple vertical of white rails and pink flowers.

Aspen flowed toward it, steady and sure. Clara counted the rhythm under her breath.

One. Two. One. Two.

They cleared it easily.

Next came the bending line. Then a soft rollback. Clara guided Aspen with gentle aids, letting him move like he knew how. He flicked an ear back at her voice when she whispered encouragement.

So far, clean.

The announcer's voice floated across the arena.

"Lovely rhythm from Aspen. Very smooth ride."

Her confidence built with every stride.

Then she saw it.

Fence six.

The oxer with the adjusted rail.

Smaller than the intimidating version on the far side, but built with the same carved wooden filler. The same shadow. The same deceptive illusion of size.

Her heartbeat spiked.

Aspen felt it.

His ears stiffened. His stride shortened half a step.

"No. Forward," Clara whispered. "You can do this."

She pushed her leg on and lifted her eyes above the oxer, focusing on the imaginary point Luke always told her to see. Breath. Rhythm. Forward.

But Aspen hesitated again as the shadow of the filler darkened the path ahead. Clara tightened her leg, steadied her contact, and prayed.

At the last stride, he committed.

He jumped.

She folded. They sailed over.

The landing was uneven, but they were safe.

A wave of relief swept through her so strong she nearly lost focus.

"Recover," she whispered to herself.

She circled to the last vertical. Aspen cleared it easily.

They crossed the finish.

Applause rippled through the crowd. Harper let out a whoop. Luke lifted a hand in a small, proud gesture.

Clara exhaled and stroked Aspen's neck. They had done it. It had not been perfect, but it had been clean.

She left the arena with her chest aching from the thudding of her heart.

As she exited, Victor Hale stepped forward, camera still in hand.

"Well done," he said. "Very brave over that oxer. We will talk later about perfecting your image for tomorrow."

Clara's breath caught.

Perfecting her image.

Not her riding.

Not her partnership.

Her image.

Before she could answer, the announcer called:

"Next in the ring, rider number seventy five, Megan Ward on Evermore."

Megan trotted in with a smile like a polished trophy.

Clara watched from the rail as Evermore cantered toward the

first jump with long, flawless strides. Megan's equitation was sharp. Flashy. Photogenic. The kind of round that made people lean closer to watch.

Clara stepped back. Her chest tightened.

Her clean round suddenly felt small.

And somewhere in the stands, Liam Carter was still watching, pen tapping, notebook open.

Clara felt overshadowed.

She tried to smile, but something inside her had already begun to crack.

———

Clara stayed near the warm up rail because moving felt impossible. Her legs held her, but she felt detached, as if her body had turned into something stiff and wooden. Aspen stood quietly at her side, blowing soft breaths that tickled her arm, but even his presence could not quiet the thudding in her ears.

Inside the arena, Megan picked up her canter, Evermore floating beneath her like a creature carved from polished bronze. They moved in harmony, the kind of harmony that photographers dream about and sponsors adore. Megan's back was straight, her hands steady, her smile bright enough to catch Victor's attention from across the ring.

Clara should not have watched. She knew that. Luke had told her a hundred times not to compare herself to other riders. But her eyes stayed locked on Megan's round, as if she were trapped under a spell.

Evermore flowed over the first vertical with a perfect bascule. Megan barely moved in the saddle. The judge leaned forward slightly, interest sharpened. A few spectators even murmured words of appreciation.

Then the second fence passed beneath them, and the third. Megan guided Evermore through the bending line like she was tracing a ribbon through the air. Every stride matched perfectly.

Every landing was balanced. The applause after their rollback was louder than anything Clara had heard yet that morning.

Luke appeared beside Clara, arms crossed as he studied Megan's form.

"She is riding well today," he said, but there was no criticism in his tone. Just honesty.

Clara swallowed. "She looks perfect."

"No one is perfect," Luke replied. "She just looks the part. There is a difference."

Clara did not respond.

Megan approached the same oxer that had made Aspen falter. Evermore pricked his ears and powered forward, legs lifting easily. The gelding did not hesitate. He soared with a flourish that made gasps ripple through the audience.

Even Victor Hale leaned forward, watching closely, camera half raised.

Megan landed with a smile wide enough to be seen from the far rail. She added an extra pat on Evermore's neck as if she knew exactly who was watching.

After clearing the last jump without a single error, Megan trotted out to enthusiastic clapping. Even a few Knightfall juniors clapped politely. Megan tossed her braid, glowing with triumph.

Clara felt something heavy sink inside her.

Victor Hale stepped closer to the in gate and clapped slowly. "Beautiful round. Very composed. Very confident." He glanced at Clara before turning back to Megan. "You understand presence. That matters."

Megan laughed lightly, brushing hair from her face. "Thank you. Evermore felt incredible."

Clara's stomach tightened. She stepped away from the rail, but movement around her seemed to press in from all sides. Riders, trainers, parents, spectators. The swirl of excitement and chatter felt louder with every passing moment.

"Clara." Luke's voice followed her. "Walk Aspen. Do not stand here."

She nodded and led Aspen away from the ring. Her legs carried her automatically, but her mind raced in circles.

Clean round. Good rhythm. A small hesitation at the oxer. One uneven landing. Not perfect. Not flashy. Not memorable.

Megan's round had been all three.

Harper caught up to her near the barn entrance. "I saw both of your rounds. Yours was lovely and hers was dramatic. Judges are not always looking for drama. You know that, right"

"I know," Clara said softly.

"And Aspen was relaxed. Evermore was almost too electric," Harper added. "He looked a little uneven again during warm up."

Clara paused. "You noticed it too."

"Only for a stride," Harper said. "But something is there."

Clara wanted to hold onto that truth. She wanted it to matter. But all she could feel was the comparison between Megan's picture-perfect confidence and her own shaky breath.

Victor's words lingered like unwelcome guests in her head.

Perfecting her image for tomorrow.

Clara shivered.

They reached Aspen's stall. She slipped the bridle off and replaced it with his halter, the simple act grounding her for a moment.

Aspen turned his head sharply as if he sensed her unraveling. His warm breath brushed her forearm, and he nudged her with such insistence that she almost dropped the reins.

"I am okay," she whispered.

He nudged again, harder this time.

"Really. I am okay."

Her voice cracked on the final word.

Harper put a hand on her shoulder. "Clara. Sit down for a minute."

"I should help with the jump resetting," Clara said.

"No. You should breathe," Harper countered.

Clara leaned against Aspen's stall door. Her breath shook in her chest, trapped under the weight of expectations. Not just her own, but Victor's, Megan's, the whispers in the stands, the scout from Knightfall, and even the stories she told herself about what a real rider should be.

Luke entered the barn with long strides and came to stand in front of her. His expression was steady, calm. It made her throat tighten further.

"You rode well," he said. "Not perfect. Not bad. Just well. That is enough."

"It does not feel like enough," Clara whispered.

"You are letting the noise get in the way. Do not let other riders live in your head."

Clara exhaled, but her breath still felt uneven. "She made it look so easy."

"Because she has never faced what you faced this winter," Luke said. "Or if she has, she hides it behind attitude and shine."

Clara blinked at that. She had never thought about it that way.

Luke rested a hand on Aspen's shoulder and then looked up at Clara again. "Listen carefully. You deserve to be here. You earned your place in this division. You do not need to compete with Megan for Victor's approval. You ride for yourself and for this horse."

Aspen lifted his head and nudged Luke as if to agree. Luke smiled faintly and scratched Aspen's cheek.

"See," he said. "He knows it too."

Clara let out a small laugh that felt more like a breath slipping free than actual humor. But it helped.

A shout from outside caught their attention.

"Next division will begin in five minutes. Riders please check in at the in gate."

Parents bustled past with jackets and helmet bags. A show volunteer hurried toward the office tent. The energy around them continued to swell as the show gained momentum.

Clara steadied herself enough to breathe normally again. She looked at Aspen's soft eyes and felt a little of her balance return.

"I want to watch the next class," she said quietly. "Just to stay in the rhythm of the show."

Luke nodded. "Good idea. But no comparing. Observe. Learn. That is all."

She followed him out of the barn with Harper trailing behind. They approached the arena where the next riders were starting to warm up.

People filled the small sets of bleachers and lined the fences. Children held snow cones. Camera shutters clicked. The judge's booth was decorated with flowers that someone had bought that morning. It was chaos wrapped in excitement.

Clara found a spot at the rail where she could see clearly. Harper stood beside her, sipping from a water bottle she had stolen from the volunteer table.

As riders cantered past, Clara listened to the conversations surrounding her.

"She looks so polished. Knightfall has really stepped up its training this year."

"There is a rumor their scout is here. He is supposed to evaluate juniors for the upcoming medal qualifiers."

"Did you hear Clara Bennett is competing again She looks good. I heard she had a terrible fall last winter."

The last whisper sliced through her.

She turned her face away from the two women speaking, her cheeks warming with embarrassment.

Harper bristled beside her. "Ignore them."

Clara nodded even though she felt the weight of their words. For a moment, she imagined the accident all over again. The sound of the other horse slipping. The scream. The thud. The surge of fear. The cold sensation of losing control. The memory tightened her lungs.

Then she forced her gaze back to the ring.

A pair of young Knightfall riders trotted past. One of them glanced briefly at Clara, then looked away. The other whispered something that made them both laugh quietly. Clara did not have to guess what the comment had been about.

Not the fall itself. But the story people built around it.

Clara steadied her breathing and watched as the next rider in the ring approached the oxer with the carved wooden filler. The horse hesitated a hair. The rider overcorrected and tapped the rail. A hollow clunk echoed across the arena.

Luke leaned slightly toward Clara. "See. Everyone has moments."

She nodded again.

But she was still replaying her own jump in her head. Aspen had hesitated. She had tightened. They had made it, but the hesitation haunted her more than a refusal would have.

A refusal would have been simple. Clear. A mistake she could correct.

The hesitation felt like a warning.

The class finished and the crowd clapped softly. Clara clapped too, though her hands felt heavy.

As she let her gaze wander across the spectators, she saw the boy again.

Liam Carter.

Sitting higher up in the stands.

Notebook open.

Pen tapping.

Eyes scanning the riders like he was cataloging strengths and weaknesses.

He paused.

Looked directly at her.

Tilted his head.

Then returned to his notes.

Clara felt a confusing mix of curiosity and irritation.

"Is he scouting us too" she whispered.

Harper shrugged. "Who knows. He is a Knightfall rider. They treat riding like a science experiment."

Clara kept watching him. There was no malice in his expression. Just focus. Study. Interest. Which somehow felt even more unsettling.

She turned away, pressing one hand lightly over her chest to calm her heartbeat.

Harper nudged her. "You should take a break. Drink water. Sit."

"I am fine," Clara said.

"You always say that," Harper replied. "And it is never true on show days."

Clara opened her mouth to argue, but a volunteer approached with a clipboard.

"Clara Bennett" the woman asked. "The show office asked me to tell you that Mr. Hale would like to speak with you for a moment near the far rail."

Clara froze. "Now"

"Yes. He asked that you come before the next division begins."

The volunteer hurried away.

Harper groaned. "You do not have to go."

"I know," Clara said. "But if he wants to talk, I should hear what he has to say."

"Be careful," Harper warned. "He is slippery."

Clara took a breath, squared her shoulders, and walked toward the far rail. Her boots crunched softly in the sand. The sun was higher now, warm on her neck. The green valley stretched behind the ring, deceptively peaceful.

Victor Hale stood waiting with his camera slung over his shoulder. His smile was polished and unreadable.

"Clara," he said smoothly. "A word."

She stopped a respectful distance away. "Yes"

"You handled yourself well today. The oxer showed your determination. Courage is valuable to a brand like mine."

"Thank you," she said, though her voice felt tight.

"You did not look entirely comfortable in the air," Victor added, his tone soft enough to pass for concern if she did not listen closely. "We will work on that. The image you present is important. Confidence. Balance. Precision."

She swallowed. "I am trying."

"I know," Victor said. "And you have potential. That is why I am watching. We will want to refine your presentation for tomorrow. There are eyes on this show. Trainers. Scouts. Media."

Clara felt cold despite the sun.

"Will you be taking more photos" she asked.

"Of course," he said. "We need to build material for the season."

The season. A single word with a dozen implications.

Clara nodded faintly.

Victor stepped closer in a way that felt casual but was not. His voice lowered.

"Clara. Do not let one strong rider shake you. Every rider has her role. You should focus on consistency. Megan provides the flair. You provide the narrative."

Her heartbeat stumbled. "Narrative"

He smiled. "Overcoming fear. Showing growth. Audiences love that. It sells well."

Clara felt suddenly hollow. Like she had become a story he wanted to control.

Victor checked his camera and turned away. "Rest up. You have more to prove tomorrow."

Clara watched him leave, feeling as if a rope had been tied around her chest and pulled tight.

Harper hurried to her side. "What did he say"

Clara shook her head. "Nothing I want to repeat."

Luke was farther down the rail, speaking with another trainer. He caught Clara's eyes, reading her expression instantly. His face tightened with concern.

She looked down at her boots before he could reach her.

"I need air," she said quietly to Harper.

Clara did not wait for a response. She walked toward the far edge of the showgrounds where a row of trees offered shade. Her breath quivered in her chest.

Aspen had done everything she asked. He had carried her through the round even when she faltered. She should have been proud.

Instead, she felt overshadowed.

By Megan's round.

By Victor's expectations.

By the whispers about her fall.

By the scout.

By the pressure of tomorrow.

She reached the shade, rested her hand against the trunk of a tree, and closed her eyes.

Just breathe, she told herself.

But it was difficult.

Very difficult.

———

Clara stayed beneath the shade of the trees until her breathing steadied. The distant sound of hooves, applause, and announcers calling rider numbers drifted toward her on the cool breeze. The showgrounds bustled with excitement and preparation, yet the small pocket of quiet she had found felt like a different world altogether.

She pressed her fingertips softly into the rough bark, grounding herself. Aspen had done everything right. She kept repeating that thought, trying to let it sink deeper than the doubt that had been swirling since her round.

He did his job.

He trusted her.

He carried her even through the moment she froze.

She needed to honor that trust, but right now her mind felt

fogged with too many voices and expectations that did not belong to her.

Footsteps approached. Slow. Careful. Familiar.

Luke.

He did not speak right away. He simply leaned beside her against the tree, leaving enough room for the silence to breathe. He always knew when to give her time.

Eventually, he said, "You walked away too fast."

Clara did not open her eyes. "I needed space."

"I know," he replied. "But you do not have to hide from me."

She took a slow breath. "I am not hiding."

"You are," he said gently. "And you are allowed to. Just not from yourself."

Clara's hands tightened around the straps of her gloves. "I did not ride like her. I did not look like her. Megan was perfect."

Luke let out a soft exhale that held both patience and understanding. "You are not Megan. You do not need to be Megan. She rides loud. You ride quiet. There is nothing wrong with that."

"Quiet does not get attention," Clara whispered.

"Attention is not the goal," Luke said. "Connection is. And rhythm. And trust. Your horse had all three."

Clara opened her eyes and stared at the sunlight flickering through the leaves. "Victor thinks my hesitation tells a story. Not a good one."

Luke's tone sharpened slightly. "Victor sees what he can market. Not what matters."

"He said we will perfect my image," Clara muttered. "Image. As if I am supposed to be a photograph."

"You are not," Luke said. "You are a rider. One who came back from something real. One who is still learning how to breathe when things get loud."

Clara felt her throat tighten again, but this time with something like relief.

"Do you think he is going to sponsor us" she asked quietly.

Luke paused, choosing his words with care. "I think Victor Hale is looking for a barn that makes him look good. If he sees something here that helps his brand, he will offer. If he does not, he will leave. That decision is not on your shoulders."

"It feels like it is," Clara admitted.

"I know it does," he said. "But it is not."

A high pitched whinny cut through their quiet. It came from the warm up ring, sharp enough to break Clara's concentration. She looked over and saw Evermore dancing sideways, neck arched, one hind leg lifting oddly again before he corrected himself. Megan's trainer snapped a cue and circled him, pushing him forward.

Something in Clara's stomach twisted.

"That leg is not right," she murmured.

"I see it," Luke replied.

"Should someone say something" Clara asked.

Luke watched Evermore for a long moment. "I will mention it to the steward quietly. They will keep an eye on it. It is not your job to fight Megan's battles."

Clara nodded, grateful he had noticed too. The horses mattered. Even when the rest of the world cared about ribbons and photos and applause.

The loudspeaker crackled overhead.

"Attention riders. Level One Junior Hunter results will be posted in five minutes."

Harper came jogging toward them, out of breath. "Clara. You placed. Not top three, but you placed. Fifth out of twenty one."

Clara blinked. "Fifth"

"Yes. Fifth." Harper beamed. "That is good. That is very good."

Clara nodded. Fifth was respectable. Solid. But the sting of Megan's round still lingered like a bruise.

Harper was still talking. "And people noticed your oxer. One woman near me said you looked brave. Brave, Clara. That is a compliment."

Clara managed a smile. "Thanks."

Harper tilted her head. "Are you okay, though You look like you might pass out or fight someone, and I cannot tell which."

Clara let out a laugh that surprised all three of them. "Neither. I am just thinking."

"Dangerous," Harper joked, nudging her lightly. "Come on. Aspen needs to cool down. And you need water that is not just the stress tearing through your bloodstream."

They walked back toward the barn. Aspen whickered when he saw her, stretching his neck over the door to greet her with a warm breath. Clara rested her forehead against his cheek for a moment, breathing in the earthy smell of his coat. Aspen's eyelids fluttered, and he leaned into her with steady comfort.

"You did so well," she whispered. "Thank you."

Aspen sighed and nibbled gently at her sleeve.

Harper stood beside them with a bottle of water. "Drink. Because I swear if you faint I will make fun of you forever."

Clara drank without argument.

Around them, the barn bustled as riders returned from their classes. The energy was electric. Whispered congratulations. Quiet disappointment. The rustle of show jackets being unbuttoned. The sharp click of hoof picks and the soft swish of fresh shavings.

Victor Hale passed through the aisle once, speaking in a low voice to one of the other trainers. His camera hung over his shoulder. His eyes flicked toward Clara for a moment, unreadable.

She glared at the ground to avoid engaging.

Harper leaned closer. "He smells like trouble."

"I know," Clara said.

Luke joined them again as Aspen finished drinking from his bucket. His expression softened when he saw the horse resting his head near Clara's shoulder, quiet and steady.

"Are you ready to watch the next division" Luke asked. "It could help take your mind off Victor's nonsense."

Clara nodded. They made their way back to the ring. A group of younger riders were warming up. Most of them were nervous. A few looked excited. The parents looked more nervous than the kids.

Clara found a spot near the rail once more. The familiar whoosh of horses passing, the murmurs of the crowd, and the rhythmic thump of hoofbeats began calming her again.

A few minutes later, motion in the stands caught her eye.

Liam Carter.

He had moved closer to the front. His pen scratched across his notebook quickly, pausing every so often as he studied a rider or whispered something to the coach beside him.

Clara's heart did an odd little jump. She did not know why. Possibly curiosity. Possibly irritation. Possibly something she did not want to name.

He looked up from his notes and met her eyes directly.

Not in a mocking way. Not like Megan. More like he was studying a puzzle that had many pieces.

Then he nodded almost to himself, wrote something else down, and continued watching the ring.

"What is his deal" Harper whispered.

"No idea," Clara said.

But she could not help glancing at him again. And again. Something about his quiet focus reminded her of Aspen. Observant. Calmer than others. Not showy. But sharp.

The next rider in the ring chipped a stride before the oxer and barely made it over. Liam jotted something quickly. Clara wondered if he was comparing riders. Wondered if he had watched her round earlier. Wondered what he had written about her.

She shook her head. Enough comparing. Enough spirals.

Luke pointed at one of the riders approaching the first fence. "See her hands. Too tight. That is why her horse is rushing. Learn from others. But do not judge yourself through their mistakes."

Clara watched closely. Studying technique felt steady. Safe. Familiar. Within her control.

After a few more rounds, the sun dipped slightly, softening the edges of the valley. The wind picked up, blowing the banners into gentle waves. The day was not over, but the energy began to shift from frantic morning rush to afternoon steadiness.

Clara exhaled and rested her hands on the fence. "Tomorrow feels bigger than I thought it would."

"It usually does," Luke said.

"Are you sure I can handle it"

"You just did," he replied. "One round at a time."

Harper nodded. "You looked strong, Clara. Not perfect. Not polished. But strong. And that matters more."

Clara let the words settle slowly. She looked toward the ring where the next rider was finishing a clean round. Applause swelled. Dust shimmered. Horses snorted and pawed. The world kept moving.

She heard Victor's comment again in her head.

Perfecting your image for tomorrow.

She pushed the words away. They had no place here.

For a brief moment, she let herself imagine the next day without comparison. Without Victor. Without Megan's perfect smile or the whispers about the accident.

Just her.

Just Aspen.

Just a course set across a bright valley.

A test she could face step by step.

Stride by stride.

The noise around her softened. The valley wind carried the sound of the creek. Aspen waited in his stall, steady as the earth beneath her feet.

Tomorrow was coming.

And despite the doubts and shadows, Clara felt the faintest spark of something she had not felt in a long time.

Hope.

8

The morning sun had barely climbed above the ridge when Luke walked the course again, clipboard tucked under his arm and a frown carved into his expression. The show ring was quiet at this hour, the only sound the soft crunch of his boots on the fresh footing. Clara followed a few steps behind, Aspen grazing on a patch of grass near the gate.

Luke stopped in front of the combination jump. The same one that had unsettled Clara yesterday. The same one that had swallowed her confidence for a few terrifying seconds.

He crouched, touched the groundline, and hissed a breath through his teeth.

"What is it" Clara asked, her pulse picking up.

"The groundline," Luke said, shaking his head. "It is wrong. Someone placed it too far under the vertical instead of out front. It creates a false takeoff point. Makes the horse guess. That is why Aspen hesitated."

Clara's breath caught. "I knew something felt off."

"You were right," Luke said. "A misplaced groundline can trick even the most honest horses. Especially sensitive ones like Aspen."

A course crew member hurried over, already looking guilty. Luke pointed at the rail. His tone was calm but firm.

"This needs to be reset correctly. And do it quietly. I do not want riders panicking before the next class."

The crew member nodded quickly. Together, they slid the groundline forward until it lay exactly where it should have been all along. The adjustment looked small. Barely noticeable. Yet the difference felt enormous.

Clara exhaled in relief. At least she was not imagining things. At least Aspen had not been the problem.

But her relief did not last long.

Footsteps clicked across the arena boards. Megan appeared, Evermore gleaming beside her. She crossed her arms and tilted her head at the jump.

"So that is the excuse," she said. "A crooked pole. Figures."

Clara felt her jaw tighten. "It was set wrong."

"Or Aspen just got overwhelmed," Megan replied sweetly. "Some horses are like that. Fragile. Sensitive. Hard to trust in big moments."

Clara bristled. Aspen snorted as if insulted.

Luke's voice remained steady but cold. "Watch yourself, Megan. A misplaced groundline can cause a fall. This is not a joke."

Megan shrugged, not looking impressed. "Evermore did not have a problem with it."

Clara opened her mouth to retort, but Luke gently touched her arm, signaling her not to take the bait.

Evermore shifted his weight. For a split second, that same odd hesitation flickered in his hind leg again. Megan yanked the reins lightly.

"Come on, boy. Do not start acting up now."

Clara exchanged a glance with Luke, who raised an eyebrow. Megan did not notice.

Before Clara could move away, Victor Hale appeared at the gate, wearing an expression of mild curiosity, as if all of this confirmed something he already believed.

"Interesting morning," he said, studying the jump. "A simple mistake, but an important one. Horses can be so unpredictable."

Luke stood straighter. "The crew fixed it. The course is fine now."

Victor nodded, but his attention drifted to Clara. "Still, that moment yesterday tells me something important. With stronger coaching and more consistent show strategy, Clara could be unbeatable."

Clara froze.

Luke's expression sharpened.

Victor smiled gently, as if making a harmless observation. "It is not a criticism. Clara has raw talent. What she needs is refinement. A rider with her story requires a coach who understands the demands of visibility."

Clara's heart landed heavily in her stomach. The implication was clear.

She met Victor's gaze. "Luke is my coach."

Victor tilted his head. "Of course he is. For now. But riders grow. They evolve. Sometimes they need more support than one small barn can offer."

Clara stiffened. "Luke is not the problem."

Victor's smile did not falter, but something sharper flickered behind his eyes. "I never said he was. But potential requires opportunity. And opportunity often requires change."

Luke stepped slightly closer to Clara in a protective motion. His tone remained calm but steady. "She does not need a different program."

Victor gave a soft hum, as if cataloging that resistance. "We will talk later, Clara. Privately. I want to discuss how we can shape your story for the season. You have something special, but the public needs help seeing it."

Clara felt her stomach twist. She did not want a meeting. She did not want her story shaped. She wanted to ride. She wanted to breathe. She wanted her confidence back.

Victor glanced at the busy showgrounds behind him. "Knightfall has been building its media presence this year. New filming crew. New youth features. Sponsors love young riders with strong personal branding."

He looked at Clara once more. "You could fit into that vision, if you are willing."

Clara swallowed hard.

Aspen stepped closer to her side, resting his warm muzzle against her arm.

Megan smirked. "Good luck with that, Clara. Some riders just have the look for media."

Clara ignored her. She kept her gaze steady on Victor even though her pulse hammered.

"I am not interested in replacing my coach," she said quietly.

Victor's smile deepened, but it did not reach his eyes. "Very well. We will revisit the topic later."

With that, he walked away. Megan followed, the picture of smug confidence.

When they were out of earshot, Clara let out a shaky breath.

Luke rested a hand on Aspen's neck. "You handled that well."

"It did not feel like it," Clara murmured.

"It was," Luke said. "Victor pushes. He looks for small cracks. Do not let him widen them."

Clara nodded. She looked again at the corrected jump, the groundline now exactly where it belonged. Aspen pawed the dirt and snorted softly, as if reminding her that he had known all along something was wrong.

"You trusted your instincts," Luke said. "Trust them again now."

Clara touched Aspen's cheek. "We are fine," she whispered.

She wanted it to be true.

Because with the course fixed and the show moving forward, the next challenge waited just ahead.

And Victor Hale was far from finished.

9

how afternoon arrived with a thick, heavy tension that clung to Clara's skin. The warm up arena buzzed with activity, but every sound felt sharper than usual. Horses snorted. Hooves struck the ground. Riders murmured instructions to each other. None of it helped.

Clara stood beside Aspen with her helmet in her shaking hands. Her second round was minutes away, and she felt completely hollow inside, as if something important had slipped out of her without warning.

Aspen sensed it instantly. His muscles twitched beneath his coat. His breathing quickened. He tossed his head and pawed once at the dirt.

Luke noticed everything. He stepped directly in front of Clara, blocking her view of the arena gate.

"Look at me," he said softly.

She tried, but her eyes darted past him toward the course. "I cannot do this," she whispered.

"Yes, you can."

"No," she said again, voice cracking. "I am shaking. I cannot breathe normally. Aspen feels it. He is going to think something is wrong."

"Something is wrong," Luke replied calmly. "You are panicking. That is not a crime. You are allowed to feel scared."

Clara squeezed her helmet tighter. "If I make a mistake again, everyone will think it is because of the fall. They will think I am weak or broken."

"You do not have to prove anything to them," Luke said.

But she could not believe him. Not today. The noise in her mind was too loud. Her pulse thudded violently against her throat.

Luke placed his hands gently on her shoulders. "Grounding exercise," he said. "Right now. Name five things you see."

Clara swallowed hard. "The banners. Aspen's mane. The judge's booth. The water bucket. The wooden gate."

"Four things you can touch."

"My reins. The saddle pad. The fence rail. Aspen's shoulder."

"Three things you can hear."

"Hooves. The announcer. Someone's zipper."

"Two things you can smell."

"Leather. Dust."

"One thing you can feel inside your chest."

Clara's breath hitched. "Fear."

Luke nodded. "Now breathe through it."

She tried. She really tried.

But the moment she inhaled deeply, tears spilled down her cheeks without warning. She pressed her face into her hands, shoulders shaking.

"Clara," Luke said softly, "it is alright. Let it out."

She stepped into the corner of the arena, away from the crowd. Aspen followed her, ears pinned back with worry. Clara leaned against his neck, sobbing into his warm coat.

"I hate this," she whispered. "I am terrified. Every time I hear the gate slam or a rail fall, I remember the accident. I cannot shut it out."

Aspen nosed her shoulder, breathing against her cheek with gentle insistence.

Luke stayed a few feet back, giving her privacy but staying near enough that she felt held.

"You are not failing," he said. "You are healing. Healing is messy."

Clara wiped roughly at her eyes.

A shift of movement behind them made her stomach drop. Megan stood near the corner, pretending to adjust Evermore's reins while very clearly listening.

Her eyes widened in false sympathy before she turned to her friend and whispered something behind her hand.

Clara's heart sank.

By the time she returned to the in gate, whispers were already spreading like wildfire.

"She is crying."

"She is still scared after the fall."

"She is not ready."

Harper glared daggers, but that did nothing to stop the ripple.

Clara mounted Aspen with trembling hands. Luke steadied her foot in the stirrup and whispered, "Ride safe. Nothing more."

She nodded. That was all she could manage.

The bell rang.

Her round was neither clean nor disastrous. Aspen hesitated at the first line, then rushed the single vertical. Clara rode defensively, hands tight, body tense. She added strides where she should have flowed forward. She chose caution over confidence at every turn.

It was not bold.

Not brave.

Not impressive.

It was simply enough to get through the course.

When she exited the ring, applause came politely but without interest.

Victor Hale waited at the rail with his camera hanging unused.

His expression was cool.

"That was very controlled," he said. "Almost too controlled. You held back. The fire was gone."

Clara's cheeks burned. "I just wanted to be safe."

"Safe does not win," he replied quietly. "Safe does not sell. We will talk later about standards."

He walked away without another word.

Clara felt the sting of disappointment far deeper than she expected.

Harper rushed to her side. "Ignore him. He does not get to decide your worth."

"It still hurts," Clara whispered.

"I know," Harper said.

Luke approached, took Aspen's reins, and touched Clara's boot. "No more riding today. You need a reset ride in the morning. Early. Before anyone watches."

Clara nodded, breathing shakily.

As she slid out of the saddle, she glanced toward the stands.

Liam Carter sat with his notebook open, watching the warm up ring again. His eyes were not on her round. They were on Aspen, studying how the gelding paced and reacted to each passing horse.

Clara did not know if that made her feel exposed or understood.

Maybe both.

She rubbed her face with the back of her glove.

She was losing herself, and everyone could see it.

Tomorrow, something had to change.

10

The showgrounds were quieting down by late afternoon. Most riders had retreated to the barn aisles to untack and regroup, but Victor Hale requested Clara meet him behind the sponsor booth near the edge of the property. The location felt intentional, tucked away from the main crowd but close enough that anyone walking by could see them.

Clara hesitated before stepping into the small tent. Aspen's soft breaths and Luke's steady presence were far behind her now. She felt exposed, stripped of the thin confidence she had been trying to rebuild.

Victor was already there, seated at a small folding table with a sleek black folder laid neatly in front of him. He gestured to the empty chair.

"Clara. Sit."

She lowered herself onto the chair, hands resting nervously in her lap.

Victor opened the folder and slid a packet of crisp papers toward her. "I wanted to speak about your future. You have potential. Real potential. But if you want to go anywhere in this sport, you must understand the cost of visibility."

Clara frowned at the contract. "What is this"

"A rider partnership," Victor said. "Exclusive representation. Appearances. Social content. Monthly features. A training schedule that aligns with our brand. In exchange, you receive full sponsorship for shows, gear, and travel."

It looked official. Heavy. More pages than she expected anyone her age to sign.

Clara flipped to the second page and felt her stomach tighten.

"This says you want control over my media posts."

"Brand integrity requires consistency," Victor replied smoothly.

"And here," she said, pointing, "It says you can approve or reject shows I attend."

"You will be representing us," he said. "Your choices reflect the company."

Clara flipped further. The deeper she read, the colder she felt.

"This is my whole life," she whispered.

"It is an opportunity," Victor corrected. "A chance to reshape your identity in a way that gains traction."

"Reshape," she repeated softly.

Victor leaned forward, eyes sharp. "You have a compelling story. A fall. A recovery. A comeback. Audiences love an underdog. But you must let us craft that narrative. A polished image sells. And you need selling power if you want to rise."

Clara closed the folder slowly. Her breath shook.

"This is not what I thought sponsorship meant."

"Every sponsorship has strings," Victor said. "The question is whether you can handle them."

Clara felt her pulse thud. She imagined her life folded into these pages. Scheduled. Scripted. Controlled.

She lifted her gaze. "What if I say no"

Victor rested his arms lightly on the table. "Then I will respect your choice. But Willow Creek may lose its shot at future sponsorship. These decisions affect entire barns, not just one rider."

Clara stiffened. "So if I refuse, you will drop Willow Creek"

"I will reconsider my investment," Victor answered simply. "I need riders who commit fully. Half hearted partnership is not partnership at all."

The air thickened between them. Clara felt pressure pressing down on every bone.

He was not just offering a contract. He was offering a sacrifice.

Her identity.

Her freedom.

And possibly her barn's future.

"You want to decide who I am as a rider," Clara whispered.

"I want to guide your potential," Victor said. "And in exchange, I expect loyalty."

Clara pushed the folder back across the table.

"I need time."

Victor nodded, but there was no warmth in the gesture. "Of course. Not long though. I have been scouting new talent this season. Young riders with hunger and momentum. You have seen some of them. Knightfall is full of promise."

Clara's breath caught. She thought of Liam Carter watching riders closely. Taking notes. Being groomed for something bigger.

Victor continued, "Talent is everywhere. Commitment is rare. Decide which you want to be."

Clara rose to her feet. Her legs felt weak. "I will think about it."

"Good," Victor said. "Your choice will reflect your ambition. And your loyalty."

Clara stepped out of the tent and into the fading light. The sky glowed soft pink above the valley, but she felt none of its beauty. Her hands shook as she hugged herself tightly.

If she said yes, she would become someone she no longer recognized.

If she said no, Willow Creek could lose everything.

Luke. Harper. Aspen. The whole team.

Her choice would ripple through all of them.

She walked back toward the barn in a daze, heart heavy with the truth she had been avoiding.

This was not about one round or one show.

This was about who she would become.

And what she would sacrifice to get there.

11

The valley was still wrapped in pale lavender light when Clara reached the arena. Dawn had softened everything. The rails looked less intimidating. The air smelled clean and cool. Even the dust seemed to settle respectfully, as if the whole world understood that this morning was meant to be quiet.

Aspen walked beside her with slow, relaxed steps. His ears flicked gently, curious but calm. Clara rested her hand on his neck and felt the steady rise and fall of his breath. The knot inside her chest loosened a little.

Luke was already waiting at the center of the arena. He held no clipboard. No poles were set. No spectators watched. He simply stood there with his hands in his pockets, shadows stretching long behind him.

"Morning," he said softly.

"Morning," Clara replied.

"Ready for a reset ride"

She nodded, though nerves fluttered inside her. "I think so."

Luke walked over and helped her tighten the girth. "Today is not about technique. Not about showing. Not about anyone else. It is just you, the horse, and the moment you are in. Nothing more."

Clara mounted slowly, settling into the saddle as if waking from a long sleep. Aspen breathed out and lowered his head, already sensing the shift in energy.

"Walk when you are ready," Luke said.

She gave Aspen a gentle squeeze. They moved forward in a soft, stretching walk. No tension. No hurry. Just rhythm.

Clara inhaled deeply. The cold morning air filled her lungs, clearing away the residue of yesterday's panic. Each step Aspen took felt like a reminder. Slow. Steady. Here.

"Good," Luke said. "Loosen your reins. Let him stretch his neck."

Clara softened her fingers and let the reins slip out an inch. Aspen responded immediately, relaxing through his back and lowering his head.

Luke stood quietly, letting the stillness settle. "Feel him," he said after a long while. "Not the course. Not the crowd. Just him."

Clara closed her eyes for a moment and felt Aspen's warmth beneath her. His hoofbeats were soft in the sand, almost like a heartbeat she could sync with. Her shoulders lowered. Her breath steadied.

They moved into a slow trot. Aspen lifted lightly, stretching into the contact. Clara let her seat follow his movement without thinking about angles or judges or anyone's expectations.

Luke moved with them, never raising his voice. "You are at your best when you ride with him, not against your fear. This is who you are."

Clara swallowed hard. A quiet ache filled her chest. Not painful. Just honest.

For the first time in days, she did not think about Megan. She did not think about Victor's contract. She did not think about whispers or scouts or flawless rounds.

She thought about the first time she ever sat on Aspen. The first time she felt what partnership meant. The first time she understood that riding was not about being perfect. It was about being present.

She slowed to a walk again, letting Aspen stretch. A warm breeze drifted through the valley, carrying birdsong and the faint scent of morning hay from the barn.

"I forgot," Clara whispered.

Luke stepped closer. "Forgot what"

"Why I love this," she said softly. "Why I ride. It is not for applause. It is not for photos. It is not for sponsorships." She looked down at Aspen, who flicked his ear as if listening. "It is for this. For him. For the moments that make me feel brave again."

Luke smiled. "Then you already know your answer about the contract."

Clara nodded slowly, the decision settling inside her with surprising clarity. "I cannot let someone turn me into a product. I want to ride for joy. Not for an image someone else controls."

"Good," Luke said. "Then that is your path."

They walked another slow circle. The rising sunlight warmed Clara's arms. Aspen blew out a long, content sigh.

Peace.

For the first time since the accident, she truly felt it.

Luke pulled out his phone and glanced at the screen briefly. "Interesting," he murmured.

"What is it" Clara asked.

"Email from Coach Amber Leigh," he said. "She is asking if Willow Creek would be open to a joint clinic with Knightfall next month."

Clara blinked. "Knightfall"

Luke nodded. "Seems like new opportunities are coming whether we want them or not."

Clara laughed softly. "I guess so."

But this time, she did not feel overwhelmed.

She felt ready.

She guided Aspen to a halt and leaned forward to hug his neck. "Thank you," she whispered into his warm coat.

Aspen nickered, leaning into her leg with quiet affection.

Luke rested his hand on Aspen's shoulder. "Tomorrow will bring whatever it brings. But this morning, you found yourself again. That matters more than any ribbon."

Clara smiled through a soft breath. "I think I needed this more than anything."

"Everyone does," Luke said. "Even the strongest riders lose their way sometimes. What matters is finding the thread again."

Clara looked out across the glowing valley. The arena no longer felt like a place of fear. It felt like home again.

And she knew exactly what she needed to do next.

She would tell Victor Hale no.

Not out of fear.

But out of freedom.

<h1 style="text-align:center">12</h1>

The afternoon sun warmed the valley as the final division gathered near the ring. The Spring Show had lasted two long days, but somehow this last round felt bigger than anything that came before it. Riders hurried past with glossy coats and polished boots. Parents whispered encouragement. Horses flicked their tails impatiently, ready to get on with the work.

Clara stood beside Aspen near the warm up gate, listening to the quiet pulse of his breathing. Her nerves still fluttered softly, but they did not choke her. Not today. The reset ride had changed something inside her. She felt steady. Present. A little scared, yes, but rooted.

Luke checked Aspen's girth one last time and looked up at her. "Ride your ride," he said. "Not Megan's. Not the one Victor wants. Yours."

Clara nodded, letting the words settle deep.

Harper bounced on her toes behind them. "You look calm. Scary calm. Hero calm. I approve."

Clara laughed and shook her head. "I do not feel like a hero."

"You do not have to," Harper said. "Just be you."

Across the arena, Megan mounted Evermore with a smile bright enough to blind someone. Her braid shimmered in the sunlight. Parents pointed her out. Trainers nodded approvingly. She absorbed every bit of it with a satisfied tilt of her chin.

A judge approached the gate and called, "Final riders, please check in. The course is ready."

Clara mounted Aspen. He lifted into the saddle as if rising to meet her. She stroked his neck gently.

"We are doing this together," she whispered.

Luke handed her the reins with a soft pat on her boot. "Go show them how you ride when no one is watching."

She breathed deeply and walked Aspen toward the in gate.

The announcer's voice echoed across the valley.

"Next entry, rider number seventy four, Clara Bennett on Aspen."

Clara stepped into the ring.

The world quieted instantly. The crowd became a blur. The fences narrowed into clarity. Aspen's ears flicked forward, alert but confident. Clara squeezed lightly, and the gelding moved into a rhythmic trot that transitioned smoothly into canter.

Fence one was a simple vertical with a line of yellow flowers. Clara counted her rhythm.

One two. One two.

Aspen leveled himself beautifully and cleared it with a soft, floating jump.

Fence two required a bending line. Clara kept her eyes up, letting Aspen shape the curve naturally. He found the distance with ease, landing balanced and forward.

Fence three came quickly after. A rolltop with blue rails. Aspen flicked his ears at it but trusted her leg and hand. He lifted neatly.

Clara exhaled slowly. No panic. No shake. Just partnership.

Then came the oxer.

The same combination that had caused her hesitation before. The wooden filler still cast a shadow across the ground, dark and familiar. But the groundline sat correctly now. The footing was smooth. Clara steadied her breathing.

"You are with me," she whispered.

Aspen sensed her resolve and lifted his frame, moving forward with bold purpose. Clara softened her hands. This time, she felt no ice in her chest. No whisper of fear clawing at her ribs.

They took the oxer with a single smooth stride. Aspen soared, landing with power and a soft huff.

A couple of spectators clapped quietly. Clara let the sound wash over her without letting it define her.

They approached the last two fences. A tight rollback, then the final vertical. Clara focused only on the rhythm of Aspen's strides and the feel of his neck beneath her hands.

The rollback required precision. She sat tall, guided Aspen with her inside leg, and watched him pivot like a dancer.

The final vertical rose ahead, framed by bright red flowers. Aspen drifted slightly left, uncertain. Clara put on her leg gently but firmly.

"I trust you," she said.

Aspen straightened, lifted, and cleared the jump with a clean arc.

They landed in perfect balance and cantered softly across the finish.

The applause came warm and strong.

Not thunderous. Not overwhelming. But sincere.

Clara slowed Aspen to a walk, patting his neck as a relieved laugh bubbled in her chest. Not perfect. Not flashy. But real.

It felt like winning.

Luke met her at the gate with sparkling eyes. "That was honest riding," he said. "I am proud of you."

"Thank you," Clara whispered. And she meant it.

Megan entered next.

The crowd buzzed with anticipation. Evermore pranced with the arrogance of a horse who knew he was admired. Megan's posture looked regal, textbook perfect. She gave Clara a long, knowing look before trotting in.

Clara stepped to the rail with Aspen beside her.

Megan's round was fast, clean, and polished. She attacked the course with confidence. Evermore jumped high, landing with showy enthusiasm. The crowd responded with louder applause. The judges nodded.

Megan finished with a dazzling smile, flipping her braid as she circled out of the ring.

Clara exhaled. She was prepared this time. Prepared to see someone else take the spotlight.

The ribbons were announced shortly after.

"Third place goes to Sofia Ramirez and Nightshade."

"Second place goes to Clara Bennett on Aspen."

Clara blinked in surprise. Second. She had placed second. Higher than she expected.

Harper squealed and hugged her. "Yes. Yes. Yes. Clara, you did it."

Clara hugged Aspen instead. "You did it," she whispered into his mane.

"And first place," the announcer continued, "goes to Megan Ward on Evermore."

Megan rode forward like a queen receiving a crown. Cameras flashed. Victor Hale clapped with a smug familiarity. Megan lifted her chin and soaked it in.

It did not sting as much as Clara expected.

It simply was.

After the ceremony, Victor approached Clara with a thin smile. He tapped the contract folder in his hand.

"So," he said mildly. "Have you decided"

Clara tightened her grip on Aspen's reins. "Yes."

Victor's eyes sharpened. "And"

"I am not signing."

Victor blinked once. Twice. His smile did not disappear, but it hardened.

"Clara, think carefully. This affects more than you. Sponsorship benefits the entire barn."

Clara breathed out slowly. "Then find someone who fits your brand. I am not that rider."

His tone cooled. "You are making an emotional decision."

Clara shook her head. "No. I am making an honest one. You expect control I do not want to give. You use pressure to get what you want. You twist praise into manipulation." She lifted her chin. "I cannot let you shape my identity."

Victor stared at her in silence.

Then, with a clipped nod, he turned away. "Very well. Willow Creek will no longer be considered for partnership."

Luke stepped beside Clara, arms crossed. "We will manage."

Victor looked back briefly. "There are many barns hungry for opportunity. Some of your young riders should consider moving if they want to rise."

Clara felt a chill, but she did not back down.

Victor walked away, phone to his ear, already scanning the crowd for his next target.

Harper muttered, "Good riddance."

Luke exhaled. "You chose integrity. That always costs something. But it is worth it."

Clara nodded. A heaviness lifted from her chest, replaced by something steadier. Something true.

The barn gathered around her later, offering smiles and encouragement. Hannah thanked her quietly for protecting the barn from a messy partnership. A few younger riders looked at Clara with admiration she did not expect.

The unity felt warm. Real.

As the sun dipped behind the hills, Clara walked Aspen along the quiet path behind the arena. Luke joined her, hands in his pockets.

"You rode with heart today," he said. "That is what I want you to remember."

Clara smiled at the horizon. "I think I finally know what winning means."

"What does it mean to you"

"Showing up," Clara said. "Riding with courage. Trusting my horse. Doing what is right even when it is hard."

Luke nodded. "Good answer."

Back near the barns, Megan loaded Evermore into her trailer. She smirked as Clara passed.

"See you at the medal qualifiers," Megan said lightly. "Try not to crack under pressure next time."

Clara simply smiled. "We will see."

Megan's expression flickered, unsure whether Clara's calm confidence was real. Then she climbed into her trailer and closed the door.

Clara turned toward Aspen, who rubbed his head against her arm as if claiming her.

Across the showgrounds, Liam Carter leaned against the rail, watching Aspen with that same curious focus as before. His notebook was open again. He wrote something, closed it, and looked up.

Their eyes met briefly.

Not unkindly. Not competitive. Just aware.

Harper joined Clara with two cups of lemonade. "Look," she said, pointing toward the bulletin board near the office.

A flyer fluttered in the breeze, pinned loosely to the cork.

Summer Medal Series

Open to junior riders

Regional qualifiers begin in June

Next to it sat another paper.

Knightfall Equestrian Center

We will be in touch

Clara felt a jolt of something. Not fear. Not pressure.

Possibility.

She brushed her hand down Aspen's neck and smiled softly.

Tomorrow would bring new challenges, new rivals, new tests.

But she finally knew who she was.

And she was ready.

COMING SOON
THE WILLOW CREEK SEASONS · BOOK 3

COMING SOON

Summer at Willowcreek Stables

Book Three of the Willow Creek Seasons Trilogy

Summer heat settles over the valley, bringing long days, shimmering trails, and a new season of challenges for Clara Bennett and Aspen. After the Spring Show reveals who she truly wants to be as a rider, Clara enters the warm months determined to rebuild her confidence on her own terms. No crowds. No sponsors. No noise. Only trust.

But Willowcreek Stables will not stay quiet for long.

A regional medal series sweeps through the county, attracting ambitious riders, tense rivalries, and the return of sharp competition. Knightfall Equestrian Center arrives with powerful horses, polished uniforms, and a young rider whose steady gaze seems to follow Clara everywhere. Liam Carter brings skill, mystery, and a talent that unsettles even Megan Ward.

When rumors surface about a dangerous jump modification, Willowcreek's unity is tested again. Clara must find her courage in unexpected moments, choosing not only what kind of rider she is, but what kind of teammate, friend, and competitor she wants to become.

Summer storms. Late night barn talks. New friendships and shifting loyalties.

And one final showdown that will force Clara to risk more than a ribbon.

Courage grows in the sunlight.

Summer at Willowcreek Stables begins soon.

BEHIND THE SCENES AT WILLOW CREEK
WHAT EVERYONE IS DOING UNTIL THE NEXT BOOK BEGINS

The week after the Spring Show felt like the valley exhaled. The banners came down. The jumps were moved back to their usual places. The show dust settled into the ground, washed clean by a soft spring rain. Willowcreek Stables returned to its everyday heartbeat, steady and familiar.

But inside that quiet rhythm, everyone carried their own thoughts forward.

Clara

Clara spent the first few mornings riding Aspen lightly on the trails. No judges. No crowds. Just soft dirt, birdsong, and the steady clop of his hooves. She rode without stirrups sometimes, letting her legs relax and her balance settle.

She also opened Victor Hale's folder one last time, rereading it slowly. Then she tore the papers in half and threw them away. The decision felt right every time she breathed.

She stuck the medal series flyer to the inside of her locker. Not as pressure. As possibility.

Aspen

Aspen enjoyed the return to normal life. Long grooming sessions.

Extra carrots from Harper. A few rolls in the mud that he seemed very proud of. Clara swore he understood that the season ahead would test them again, but for now he simply rested, watching the barn with soft eyes and a quiet strength.

Luke

Luke cleaned the tack room on a quiet Tuesday afternoon. He rearranged the shelves, fixed a squeaky hinge on the outer door, and replied to Coach Amber Leigh's email about the joint clinic.

He did not tell Clara yet, but he reread her round comments three times. He wanted to help her grow without ever letting pressure take her joy again.

He also kept a watchful eye on Evermore's strange hind step. Experience told him that story was not over.

Harper

Harper took photos of everything: Clara and Aspen on the trail, the early summer flowers near the creek, a row of muddy paddock boots lined up against the wall. She planned to make a show recap slideshow for the whole barn, with music that she insisted must be dramatic.

She also kept an eye on Clara. Whenever Clara withdrew into her thoughts, Harper supplied hot chocolate or sarcasm. Both helped.

Megan Ward

Megan left Willowcreek with a bright smile and her first place ribbon pinned neatly to her jacket. But once home, she replayed Clara's last round more times than she admitted. Something about the way Clara rode had changed. It bothered her.

She trained harder that week. Higher jumps. Sharper turns. Evermore protested once or twice with that odd hind step, but Megan ignored it.

She circled the date of the medal qualifiers in her planner.

Liam Carter

Liam returned to Knightfall after the Spring Show with a folder full of notes. He wrote down observations on rider posture, warm up patterns, horse behavior under pressure, and one name he had underlined twice:

Aspen

sensitive. brave. rider improving fast.

He did not show that page to anyone.

Knightfall Equestrian Center

The facility buzzed with early summer ambition. New banners. Fresh footing. A rumor of a regional scout returning soon. Coaches discussed which riders would make the strongest medal teams.

Clara Bennett's name came up in one meeting. Quietly. Curiously. Not as a competitor to dismiss, but as one to watch.

Willowcreek Stables

The barn family settled into their usual routines. Evening rides. Weekend chores. Soft conversations near the tack room door. They knew the sponsorship had slipped away, but the relief outweighed the loss. No one wanted strings attached.

One rainy Wednesday, Hannah pinned a new sheet to the bulletin board:

Summer Medal Series Schedule

Training Signups Begin Next Week

Clara stood in front of it for a long time.

Not afraid.

Not pressured.

Just thoughtful.

Her hand drifted to Aspen's mane as he nudged her shoulder gently.

Summer was coming.

And with it, challenges she could not yet name.

But this time, she was ready to meet them.

CLARA'S SHOW DAY CALMING COOKIES

A Note from Clara

I baked these the night before the Spring Show when everything inside me felt too loud.

Luke calls them calming cookies. Harper calls them bribe cookies.

Aspen tries to steal them, so they must smell good.

They are simple and soft and taste like early mornings at Willowcreek.

I make them when I need to breathe a little slower.

You can bake them before a show, before a test, or on days when courage feels far away.

I hope they help you the way they helped me.

Clara's Show Day Calming Cookies

1 cup rolled oats
1 cup flour

1 teaspoon cinnamon
1 teaspoon baking powder
A pinch of sea salt
1 egg
1 teaspoon vanilla
3 tablespoons honey
3 tablespoons melted butter
3 tablespoons warm milk
Chocolate chips or chopped nuts if you want them

Mix everything gently.
Bake at 170 Celsius for about 12 to 14 minutes.

Eat while warm if you need comfort.
Eat cold if you are on the way to the in gate.
(Do not forget to breathe between bites.)

Your horse loves you even when you are nervous.
Ride for the feeling, not the ribbon.
See you in the summer.
Clara